D0829898

"IRRESISTIBLE!"

—*The New York Times Book Review*

"Terrific book. . . . Gleams like the rarest of literary gems: a cross-generational supersmash . . . The book has everything."

—*Ft. Worth Star Telegram*

"Can't miss. . . . May well prove to be the most popular love story of the season."

—*John Barkham Reviews*

"A novel superior to Erich Segal's *Love Story*."

—*King Features Syndicate*

"Like eating a sinfully rich dessert."

—*Library Journal*

SIX WEEKS

POLYGRAM PICTURES PRESENTS
In Association with PETER GUBER and JON PETERS

DUDLEY ◆ MARY TYLER
MOORE ◆ MOORE

"SIX WEEKS"

Introducing
KATHERINE HEALY

Music Composed and Performed by
DUDLEY MOORE

Based on the novel by
FRED MUSTARD STEWART

Screenplay by
DAVID SELTZER

Produced by
PETER GUBER and JON PETERS

Directed by
TONY BILL

From PolyGram Pictures   A Universal Release
* * * * * * * * * *   © 1982 UNIVERSAL CITY STUDIOS, INC.

PG | PARENTAL GUIDANCE SUGGESTED ⊂⊃
SOME MATERIAL MAY NOT BE SUITABLE FOR CHILDREN

SIX
WEEKS

Fred Mustard Stewart

BANTAM BOOKS
TORONTO · NEW YORK · LONDON · SYDNEY

to Joan

*This low-priced Bantam Book
has been completely reset in a type face
designed for easy reading, and was printed
from new plates. It contains the complete
text of the original hard-cover edition.*
NOT ONE WORD HAS BEEN OMITTED.

SIX WEEKS

*A Bantam Book / published by agreement with
Arbor House Publishing Company*

PRINTING HISTORY

*Arbor edition published October 1974
Doubleday Book Club edition published March 1976
Doubleday Compact Book Club edition published March 1877
Bantam edition / December 1977*
*2nd printing .... December 1977   3rd printing ..... December 1977
4th printing ..... December 1982*

*All rights reserved.
Copyright © 1976 by Fred Mustard Stewart.
Cover art copyright © 1982 by Universal City Studios, Inc.
This book may not be reproduced in whole or in part, by
mimeograph or any other means, without permission.
For information address: Arbor House Publishing Co.,
235 E. 45th Street, New York, N.Y. 10017.*

ISBN 0-553-22981-8

Published simultaneously in the United States and Canada

Bantam Books are published by Bantam Books, Inc. Its trademark, consisting of the words ''Bantam Books'' and the por-
trayal of a rooster, is Registered in U.S. Patent and Trademark
Office and in other countries. Marca Registrada. Bantam
Books, Inc., 666 Fifth Avenue, New York, New York 10103.

PRINTED IN THE UNITED STATES OF AMERICA

O   13 12 11 10 9 8 7

SIX
WEEKS

Chapter
1

When I first met Charlotte Dreyfus, I had no idea
something was wrong. I often think of that August afternoon in East Hampton: the big rhododendron bushes, the green lawn, the lovely,
sprawling gray house, the shimmering turquoise
pool, the people milling about murmuring Hamp-
tons and New York gossip—the setting had an
almost Manet flavor, or perhaps the flavor of one
of those Boudin shore scenes that Charlotte had
hanging in her incredible apartment. Lovely people by the sea, a few puffy clouds skidding across
an azure sky. The sun. Summer. Tranquillity.

How pleasant it seems in retrospect; and how unlikely that death was there too.

It was a hot Saturday afternoon, and I was
campaigning for the Democratic senatorial nomination. People aren't exactly riveted by politics
in August—particularly in a non-election year—
but I was a dark horse, the New York Democratic Committee was probably not going to en-
dorse me the next spring, and if I was to have
any chance for the nomination I had to start
early enough to work up some excitement for an
upstate four-term congressman whose major
claim to fame was his "maverick" voting record
in Congress. "Maverick" in my case meant that I
had been against the Vietnam War when John-
son was still throwing in the Marines, and that I
wasn't a "classic" Democrat because I've always
been suspicious of the let's-set-up-another-federal-
agency-to-solve-the-problem-mentality that has
been so prevalent in Congress since the early
sixties. I've seen too many federal agencies foul
up to believe they're the answer to anything except lack of chaos. Well, this attitude hadn't en-
deared me to my party, but it seemed to impress
my upstate constituents enough for them to keep
electing a Democrat in a basically Republican
district. And in the post-Watergate summer of
'75, the mood of the country was so anti-Wash-
ington that, luckily for me, Bill Dalton was beginning to look less like a maverick and more
like someone who had been listening to the
voters. For this I don't claim any special wisdom

or virtue. But I do think a congressman is supposed to be a public servant, not, as so many of
my colleagues much too easily come to think, a
public master; and part of our job is to listen,
not just talk. I'd been listening for a long time,
and what I'd heard had not been flattering to
the federal government.

So I had something going for me, and there
were some people who not only thought I wasn't
crazy to try for the Senate but that I actually had
a fighting chance. One of these was a stock-
broker named Arnold Stillman, and Arnold had
volunteered to give a fund-raising party for me
at his summer house in East Hampton. Well,
when you're known as an anti-big-government
type and you're addressing a group of well-heeled
resort people, the obvious approach is to attack
federal spending, right? But as I said, I'm a maverick ("suicidal," my campaign manager calls it).
And when Arnold introduced me beside his pool,
instead of kissing the checkbooks of the rich, I
talked about the plight of the poor. The last thing
people wanted to hear about on a hot afternoon,
admittedly, but I felt these people *should* hear it. I
said a rich country like America has an obligation to give everyone a decent standard of living,
that the welfare system was riddled with abuses
and that if I were elected to the Senate I would
work for passage of a national Minimum Income
Bill—a notion that had once been popular, but
had since fallen into the political garbage can.
The parked Mercedes and Rollses shimmered

ominously in the heat, but the speech received a good reception. True, a good many of Arnold's friends could be classified as Limousine Liberals, but even for them the Minimum Income idea was as dated as last year's hemline, so the fact that they applauded surprised me. Anyway, afterward I milled about the yard, being introduced by Arnold. I passed from group to group, spending a few minutes with each, trying to be intelligent and friendly, which isn't so easy when it's over ninety-five degrees. Suddenly Arnold said in a low voice, "Here's someone you ought to meet: Charlotte Dreyfus. She owns Marguerite Dreyfus Cosmetics. Ever hear of her?"

"The face cream queen? Sure."

"She's not the type to be interested in politicians, which was why I was surprised when she came over. She lives next door. Be *nice*. If she likes you, she could write some heavy checks."

He led me to a striking-looking woman who was standing in front of a big rhododendron bush, sipping white wine and eyeing me. She was nearly as tall as I (I'm six feet two), fashionably thin with a beautiful, tanned face and blond hair. I guessed she was also about my age—forty— though she could have passed for thirty, her skin was so young. She had large gray eyes and a well-bred face. She was dressed slightly more formally than the other women in this resort crowd, wearing a white chiffon dress and a strand of pearls around her neck. She looked composed and smart, and my first impression was that here was one tough lady. Like most first impressions, it was only partly right.

"Charlotte, meet Congressman William Hartfield Dalton," said Arnold. "Bill, Charlotte Dreyfus."

She smiled and put out her hand.

"Delighted to meet you, congressman. And you surprised me."

"How?"

"Well, the last thing I thought you'd talk about in Gucci and Pucci country would be poverty politics. My daughter's right—you've got guts."

Arnold purred.

"Do you think I'd back a loser?" he said. "I'm telling you, Bill's the first Democrat we've had in years who can take the Senate seat. He's got the Republicans really worried. Hell, just two days ago I was lunching with one of them and he *admitted* they're worried in Albany—"

"Arnold," interrupted Charlotte coolly, "if there's anything I hate, it's being 'sold.' "

Which made me smile. It takes a good deal to shut Arnold up, but Charlotte had done it. She looked back at me and said, "Could I ask a favor of you?"

"Sure."

"My daughter's a great fan of yours. She couldn't come to this because I made her go to her cousin's birthday party, but she made me swear a blood oath I'd ask you over for a drink later on so she could meet you. You could hardly say 'no' to an eleven-year-old fan, could you? It's just over there."

She nodded in the direction of a line of trees.

"Bill'd *love* to come," prompted Arnold. "Wouldn't you, Bill? Betty and I have nothing planned after this, and Charlotte's got a pool. You could take a swim . . ."

"Yes, bring your bathing suit. We can take a swim and you can tell Nicky how you have all the answers to America's problems. Will you come?"

"Of course," said Arnold.

"I asked the congressman."

She looked at me as Arnold silently mouthed "money" at me over her shoulder. Now, I come from a small town on the Erie Canal—West Schuyler—where the rich, particularly New York City rich, are viewed with glinty-eyed suspicion. It's an attitude eight years in the House and four campaigns haven't led me to alter. The rich *can* be as altruistic as you or me, but the chances are they won't be, and when a politician gets a donation from an individual, he's got to be a fool if he doesn't look for a few attached strings. On the other hand, at this point I had raised a little over $40,000 toward a goal of $150,000, so I needed Arnold and I needed as many thousand-dollar contributions as I could possibly get—which was why I was in East Hampton. But that old suspicion of the rich was still in my head, and I was wondering if there weren't more to this

cosmetics queen's invitation to a drink and swim
than merely meeting her probably spoiled daughter. She might want me to reduce the taxes on
lipstick, she might want to be the next ambas-
sador to Andorra—I told myself to be on guard.
Still, she interested me. So I said, "I'd be glad to
come. I'd like it better if eleven-year-olds had the
vote, but maybe I can get yours."

She smiled. And that was how it started.

I was spending the night at Arnold's, so after the guests left he filled me in on Charlotte
and her legendary mother, Marguerite Dreyfus.
The saga went something like this: Marguerite
had come to New York from Paris at the end
of the First World War, bringing with her a perfume she had concocted in her kitchen (or so she
told the press). She had a will of iron and the
personality of a steam locomotive. Within five
years she had built up a successful perfume business. In the mid-twenties she branched into
cosmetics, and the result was the Marguerite
Dreyfus cosmetics empire—face creams, pow-
ders, lipsticks, hair conditioners. . . . The money
poured in, and Marguerite lived like a Rothschild.
She collected jewels and husbands, hanging on to
the former but going through five of the latter. In
the middle thirties she finally had her only child,
Charlotte. Charlotte grew up in the lap of fabled
wealth: the Fifth Avenue triplex, the Long Island
estate, the Florida yacht. But true to form, when
she got to her teens she rebelled against it all.

After a fight with her mother, she stormed out
of the triplex, took a tiny apartment in the Village and announced she was going to become a
sculptor. She ended up in Paris, where she fell in
love with an existentialist whom she lived with
and finally married. Though her only child,
Nicole, was a result, the marriage didn't work.
Reverting to her maiden name, Charlotte took
Nicole back to New York. She managed to patch
up her fight with her mother, but the last thing
anyone expected was for her to go into business.
Except that's exactly what happened. When Marguerite died in 1966, Charlotte took over the business. To everyone's surprise, she poured the same
enthusiasm into face cream that she had into sculpture. Sales boomed. Arnold summed it up: the one
consistent thing about Charlotte Dreyfus was her
inconsistency. She liked to surprise people.

A little before seven I went up to my room
and changed into my bathing trunks. I was hot
and tired, and the idea of a swim was welcome.
Pulling on a shirt, I went back down and started
across the lawn toward Charlotte's house. It was
separated from Arnold's property by a row of
tall trees and low bushes, but I found a clear
space and went through. The house was one of
those charming East Hampton places—brown-
shingled, white-shuttered and rambling. It was
large without being overwhelming, and the
grounds were beautifully planted. As I approached
the rear of the house I saw a young girl standing

on the diving board of the pool. She rose on her toes, then executed a graceful dive into the water. It was a lovely sight in this lovely setting, and I guessed this was my fan, Charlotte's daughter. By the time I reached the edge of the pool, she was climbing out. She was as beautiful a child as I had ever seen, with dark hair and huge violet eyes. She was a little thin, but her body was well formed, and I remembered Arnold had told me she studied ballet. When she saw me, her mouth opened slightly and she gawked.

"Oh my God," she said, "you're even sexier than you are on TV! I think I may *faint* with ecstasy! Are you for Child Lib?"

"Is child lib what I think it is?"

"Children are the last exploited minority. We're tyrannized by Adult Fascists like my mother and denied the vote and constitutional guarantees. If you come out for Child Lib, I'll work for your campaign for free, even though philosophically I'm against all forms of government."

"You mean you're a nihilist?"

"Of course. Isn't everybody? I'm Nicky, the crazy daughter. My real name's Nicole, but . . ." She sighed. "You know, you really *are* dreamy looking."

"You're not so bad yourself."

"Oh, thanks for lying about it, but I know the hideous truth. I'm too young. I'm at that awful age—all lust and no action. Yuck. I'm glad mother asked you over. Did you like her?"

"Well, we've hardly met—"

"Oh, you *will* like her. She's super, even though she's an Adult Fascist. Why do you want to be a senator?"

"Believe it or not, I think I can help people better in the Senate."

"Oh, come on. You mean you're not power-mad, like Nixon?"

"Well, maybe I'm a little power-mad. But I think politicians can do some good . . . though I'll admit that lately it makes you wonder."

She cocked her head and eyed me.

"You know," she said, "I actually believe you. I think most politicians are finks, but you couldn't be a bad guy."

"Why?"

"Because you're so gorgeous! When you were on the David Susskind Show last week, I just flipped! Would you believe I went over and kissed my Sony?"

"Today I'd believe anything."

She looked at me rather shyly.

"Do you think I could kiss you instead of my Sony? It would really give me a kick. I've never kissed a politician before. Most of them look like Lon Chaney in 'Phantom of the Opera.'"

"Well," I laughed, "I haven't sawed down many chandeliers lately, so why not?"

"Wow!" she exclaimed, running to me. "Sex City!"

She stopped in front of me, closed her eyes,

raised her face and pursed her lips as her wet bathing suit dripped all over my feet. I leaned down and kissed her. She opened her eyes and sniffed.

"What's wrong?" I said.

"That was sort of a bubblegum kiss, but I guess it's better than Ronald Reagan. Are you going swimming?"

"Sure."

"Come on, the water's super! Wait, first you've got to see my special dive!"

She ran around the pool and climbed back on the diving board. Putting her arms over her head in a graceful balletic stance, she yelled, "Watch! This is a dive I invented! It's called the Nicky Dreyfus Fouetté Dive, and some day I'm going to do it from a diving board eight hundred feet high, wearing nothing but a big light bulb in my navel! I'll be a sen-*say*-tion!"

She raised one leg, then twirled gracefully on the other, making two complete turns. Then she flipped onto her hands, walked upside down on them to the end of the board and, as I held my breath, proceeded to do a double flip in the air, breaking just in time to knife cleanly into the water.

As she surfaced she grinned and said, "Wasn't that terrific? Aren't I sen-*say*-tional?"

"You're sen-*say*-tional, and I'm jealous."

"Oh, I'll bet you could do it if you tried. You look like a jock. Oh oh. Here comes mother. She'll tell me to stop showing off and be more polite."

I looked up to see Charlotte Dreyfus coming toward us, wearing a one-piece black bathing suit, which showed off her figure to be sen-*say*-tional.

"I see you've met the Child Monster," she said. "Has she been showing off?"

"A little, but she's good. She deserves to show off."

"Don't encourage her." She looked at Nicky, who was swimming toward us. When she reached the side of the pool her mother said, "So, what do you think of the congressman?"

"I want to go to bed with him."

Charlotte gasped.

"Nicky, now cut that out! You're embarrassing!"

"I was just kidding . . ."

"If you can't behave like a civilized human being around grownups, then you can go back to the Child Ghetto. *Now*."

Nicky made a face.

"Oh, all right. I'll behave."

"That's better." Her mother turned to me. "I apologize. All the kids her age think it's smart to talk dirty—"

"*You* talk dirty!" piped up Nicky. "I heard you call Sally Ryan a lying bitch on the phone this morning."

Charlotte sighed.

"All right, Super-Brat, that blew it. Out of the pool and into the house."

"Oh, Mother . . ."

"I said *out*."

Nicky glared.

"Adult Fascist," she growled, then scrambled out of the pool and came over to me. "I apologize for Mother," she said. "She can't help it if she's hopelessly out of date. And thanks for coming over. It was super meeting you."

"Nicky," said Charlotte, "I'm sick of that word 'super.' "

Nicky looked at her with cool dignity.

"Then what, might I ask, do you suggest I use in its place?"

"Try 'nice.' "

" 'Nice' is a bland cliché." She sniffed haughtily, then turned to me and whispered, "Come back at midnight and help me escape . . ."

"Nicky!"

"I'm going. *Ciao*."

Blowing me a kiss, she started toward the house. When she reached the end of the pool, she turned and yelled, "SUPER!" Then, giggling, she scurried into the house.

"Well," sighed Charlotte, "you've met the Dream Child. Shirley Temple, as you can plainly see, she ain't."

"I like her," I said truthfully.

"Really?"

"Really."

"She's so spoiled, and it's my fault. I'm too indulgent . . ."

"Listen, I'm a pretty indulgent parent too, but my son turned out all right. She will too.

You'll see. And, if I may say so, she's going to be a knockout . . . like her mother."

She looked pleased at that.

"Thanks for both of us." She hesitated. "Well, since you were nice enough to come over, I owe you a swim and a drink. Which would you like first?"

I dove into the water, and she followed. We had both swum two laps when we surfaced in the middle of the pool.

"Who's Sally Ryan?" I asked.

"A model who's done a series of ads for us. She swore to me she's off the sauce, and this morning she called up drunk. All I need is a face identified with my products that's swelling up like a wino's."

"So you *did* call her a lying bitch?"

She hesitated, then smiled slightly. "Yep. And she is." We laughed together.

Chapter
2

We did four more laps, then pulled ourselves out.

"You're in good shape," she said, taking a towel off a sunning chair to dry her hair. "Are you a health nut like Proxmire?"

"I'm a tennis nut, and I jog. The voters don't trust paunchy politicians any more."

"I'm pretty good at tennis. How about a game tomorrow? I have a court over there."

She nodded toward the end of the house. On the side lawn, surrounded by bushes, I saw a tall tennis fence.

"I'd love it, but it has to be in the morning. I have to be in New York tomorrow afternoon."

"More politicking?"

"That's right. I'm giving a speech in Harlem." She looked surprised.

"You *are* gutsy," she said. "What are you going to talk about?"

"The same thing I talked about this afternoon —the need to get rid of the welfare system and put in something that works. I want to try my ideas out on the people who have the biggest stake in welfare—those who get it."

"It's a good idea." She hesitated a moment, looking at me, and I wondered what she was thinking. I was thinking how extremely beautiful she looked in the soft evening light. Finally she said, "How about that drink?"

"I wouldn't say no."

She picked up a bronze Chinese bell from a white table and rang it, then sat down in a pool chair.

"It was really nice of you to come over."

" 'Super,' " I corrected, sitting next to her. " 'Nice' is a bland cliché."

"Right. It was super of you to come over— particularly to please my daughter."

"That wasn't the only reason. I also came over because Arnold hopes you'll write a check for my campaign."

She smiled.

"I realize that. And perhaps I will. Particularly since you're being honest about why you're

here. You made it on your own, didn't you? I
mean, you put yourself through college, law school
. . . the whole number."

"Horatio Alger all the way."

"Don't knock it. It's to be admired. You seem
to be bright, you're articulate, and you're at least
ten times better looking than Ramsey Clark . . .
so maybe I just will write that check."

A tall man in a white jacket came out of the
house. "You rang, Miss Dreyfus?"

"Yes, Clyde, I'd like some white wine. What
about you, congressman?"

"The same, please."

"And Clyde, turn on the lights, will you,
please?"

He nodded and went back in the house. She
said, "Clyde's my chauffeur-bodyguard-butler.
He's a former wrestler and has his Black Belt,
so don't try and attack me."

"I won't if you promise to stop calling me
'congressman.' The name's Bill."

"All right, Bill." The turquoise pool suddenly lit up. Then on blinked two antique carriage
lamps attached to the house. "By the way," she
went on, "where's your wife? Doesn't she campaign with you?"

"Not if she can help it. Peggy isn't particularly fond of politics."

"Oh? But doesn't that . . . I mean, isn't the
candidate's wife always supposed to be there, smiling?"

"If you're trying to say Peggy's feeling

doesn't especially make for a campaign asset, I suppose you're right. But it's Peggy's right to do what she wants."

At which point Clyde brought out the white wine, and the subject was dropped. It's something I usually don't like to discuss anyway, Peggy's dislike of politics having become an item of contention between us. But oddly, then I wanted to discuss it with Charlotte. I had a feeling she would be a good listener. More important, a sympathetic one. Finally, though, I decided not to.

I had just taken a first sip of the excellent wine when I heard what sounded like jungle drums. I looked up at a second-floor window, which was where the noise seemed to be coming from.

"It's Super-Brat," sighed Charlotte. "Like an idiot I gave her some bongo drums." She clanged the Chinese bell and called out, "Nicky, stop it!"

Silence. She replaced the bell on the table. "She's just trying to get attention. She'll do anything for attention. In case you hadn't noticed, she's a ham."

"I noticed. What about her father?"

"He was my first husband, one of the most gorgeous men I ever saw. I absolutely drooled every time I looked at him. I thought he was the Classic French Lover. Besides that, he was an existentialist, and of course that did it. I was in my artist-intellectual period then. Well, mother warned me. I should have listened."

"What happened?"

"Existentialists booze. He'd write a chapter of the Great French Novel a year, and the rest of the time, glug glug glug. I took a chapter and a half of that and finally left. But I got Nicky out of it, so I can't really complain."

"Does she see him?"

"She used to. I'd take her to Paris at least twice a year, and she spent time with him. He'd switched to writing science fiction novels, which Nicky adored. She still does. She's very loyal to him."

"What do you mean, she 'used' to see him?"

"He died last year of alcoholism."

I started to say something, when I saw a strange figure coming out of the house behind her. I sat up, staring.

"Speaking of science fiction . . ." She turned to look. An ethereal Nicky in a white nightgown had materialized out of the house onto the terrace. She was barefoot, her arms extended straight in front of her, like a sleepwalker. In one hand she carried a lighted candle, in the other a pair of scissors. She walked slowly toward us, her eyes glazed, as if in a trance.

"It's the Zombie number," said Charlotte wearily. "I took her to Haiti last Christmas, and she never got over it."

Nicky spoke in a sepulchral tone:

"I hear the jungle drums, O Master, and I obey your summons. We are the Living Dead, doomed to walk the earth by night, mindless creatures with no will save that of the Zombie Master."

"I'll buy the 'mindless' bit," announced Charlotte. "And *this* Zombie Master says, go back up to your room and stop bothering us."

"You are not my Zombie Master, Clyde is my Zombie Master, and he has commanded me to obtain a lock of the congressman's chest hair . . ."

"Huh?" I said, staring at the scissors.

"Nicky, you're revolting. Now, *stop* it."

". . . a lock of the congressman's chest hair so we can make a Zombie Doll of him and control him when he becomes a senator. That way, Zombies will rule the world !"

"Zombies *already* rule the world," snapped Charlotte. "The idea is to get someone in the Senate who's alive. Now, put down those scissors before you hurt someone."

She was standing over me, holding out the candle and the scissors, staring at me with bulging eyes.

"Do you deny the power of the Zombie Master?" she intoned.

"No, but I'd rather hang on to my chest hair."

"Do you deny the power of Baron Samedi?"

"Who?"

"He's the devil in Haiti," explained Charlotte. "Nicky, if you don't cut out this dumb act, there's going to be big trouble."

"There already is big trouble," she said, turning. "My Zombie Master is calling me back.

There is an uprising of the Humanoids. They are attacking our graves! I must go home to fight them before my tomb is defiled."

"My God, do you have to be so gruesome—"

"Being dead is gruesome," said the Zombie, heading back to the house. "But so is being alive. *Everything* is gruesome. They don't show 'Creature Feature' on Channel Five any more. Death isn't worth living. Good night. I return to my grave."

And she vanished inside the house. I grinned at Charlotte. "She's a wild one," I said.

"Oh, she's more than a little bonkers."

She picked up the wineglass and took a drink. She was frowning as if troubled by something. Then she set the glass back down and stared for a moment at the glowing pool.

"Is something wrong?" I asked.

"No, it's . . ." She looked at me, and I was surprised how tense her face had become. "Would you excuse me?" she said. "I'm not feeling very well."

"Of course. Is there something I can get you?"

"No, really. I'll be all right. I think it was Arnold's pâté—they may have kept it in the sun too long." She got to her feet and forced a smile. "Thanks for coming over. I'll see you in the morning for tennis?"

"What time?"

"Nine?"

"I'll be here."

I watched her go in the house. Then I finished my wine and walked back to Arnold's. I suppose if Charlotte had been a person who tries for easy sympathy she would have told me then what was agonizing her, rather than waiting. But that wasn't her style; she might not have told me at all if she hadn't been so desperate for help.

For I was soon to learn the reason Nicky's "zombie" act had so devastated her mother. Charlotte had just found out that her daughter had only six weeks to live.

Chapter
3

Comes the Bicentennial, I'll be the first to light the candles on the cake, because I'm a real booster for America. I know we've done some terrible things —Vietnam is only the most obvious—and we're far from perfect; but what other country is as rich and as free as we are? In how many other countries could a farmer's son like myself have had the opportunities I've had? Not many. That's why I love this country and respect its institutions. Including marriage.

As I walked back to Arnold's house, I was thinking about marriage. Mine, to be blunt. Peggy. We met in high school in those dear, departed fifties days when making out meant kissing and heavy stuff was getting your hand inside a girl's bra. All pretty antediluvian now (there's even been a nostalgia boom for the fifties) but then? Well, Peggy was the first girl I ever fell in love with, and at the time it was passionate, heady and beautiful. Her father was an important man in West Schuyler. He owned the movie theater, built the first supermarket and had even been the mayor. He probably would have tried for the state senate, except for his stroke. I've often suspected this was the deeper reason behind Peggy's dislike of politics . . . her feeling that if her father hadn't gotten so involved with the pressures of Town Hall, become ambitious, maybe there'd have been no stroke . . . Who knows . . . ?

Peggy and Bill, the perfect young couple. Bill and Peggy, the not-so-perfect not-so-young couple. Eighteen years of marriage, the last eight of them spent in a perpetual commute between Washington and West Schuyler, big time and small town, power city and power base. Skeptical as I am about a lot that goes on in Washington, I admit I still love the place: it excites me. Peggy hated it from the first. She hated the jockeying for power, the small parties with their endless gossip, the big official receptions with *their* endless gossip. In fairness to her, at first she tried. She tried very hard. She worked on my first two campaigns and kept her complaints to a minimum. But by the third campaign she was practically invisible. Also, she was spending less time in Washington and more in West Schuyler, where her heart was and always had been. At first it was awkward. I complained. We adjusted. I still loved her and, as I'd begun to tell Charlotte, I didn't want to force her into something she genuinely didn't like. But now it was different. Now I wasn't campaigning only in my district, where I was known; I was campaigning all over the state, trying to make myself known. People wanted to see the candidate's wife. Now it was becoming more than awkward.

I went to my room, took off the wet trunks, showered and dressed. Before going down to dinner I flopped onto the bed and called home. My son answered. Jeff is seventeen and a fine-looking boy. His interests are girls, basketball, girls, conservation, girls, films, girls, and Country and Western. His private pantheon is an odd mixed bag: Walt Frazier, Ansell Adams, Federico Fellini, Jack Nicholson, Ralph Nader, Bob Denver, Ken Russell (we definitely part company there), Monty Python—and, I think, me. He's a wonderful son whom I love and am proud of. He has told me at different times he wants to be a forest ranger, a film director and/or a pro basketball player. I have no doubt he'll be a smash at whatever he does.

"It's the Great Democratic Hope," I said.

"Hi, Great Democratic Hope. How's the campaign trail?"

"Hot. What's going on?"

"Not much. I'm taking Betty to see 'Tommy.' "

"Who's Tommy?"

"Hey, dad, I thought I told you you've got to keep up? It's the new Ken Russell movie. It's a Rock opera and it's crazy. Ann-Margret gets swamped with baked beans vomiting out of a TV set."

"Sounds lovely. I take it that's a satiric comment on our society?"

"What else?"

"Okay. Whatever. Anyway, have fun. Is your mother there?"

"Hold on."

In a minute Peggy came on.

"Guess what?" she opened. "The dishwasher broke again."

"Oh, hell. Did you call Mr. Carlson?"

"Yes. He's coming some time Monday to look at it. When we get his bill, can we throw ourselves on the mercy of the Consumer Protection Agency?"

"Either that or debtor's prison. How are you otherwise?"

"Hot. How was Arnold's party?"

"Pretty good. We raised about twenty-eight hundred."

"Oh, darling, that's wonderful."

"No it isn't, but anyway. I miss you."

"And I miss you."

"Guess where I was for drinks just now."

"Let's see . . . Buckingham Palace?"

"Close. Charlotte Dreyfus'."

"You're kidding! *The* Charlotte Dreyfus? Is she making a donation?"

"Maybe."

"What's she like?"

"All warts and a moustache."

"Fat chance. I've seen her picture in *Vogue*. She's gorgeous. Should I be jealous?"

"If you were here you'd know you wouldn't have to ask that."

There was a moment's silence.

"Well, I'm not there, so I'm asking."

"She's nice. She asked me over so her daughter could meet me. I thought maybe she was angling for a political favor, which shows how suspicious *I* am. Anyway, what do you hear from the television people?"

"They'll have the cameras set up by three Monday afternoon—just in time to get Mr. Carlson on tape as he floods the kitchen."

"That should get me consumer sympathy, if nothing else. I'll be home about one-thirty."

"Okay."

"I miss you, Peggy."

"And I miss you."

"I wish you were with me."

"You said that, Bill." Her tone was measured. "Listen, I told you if you *really* need me at these damned things, I'll come. But you said you really didn't need me at Arnold's, so why try and make me feel guilty now—"

"Peggy, I'm not trying to make you feel guilty . . ."

"Oh come on, Bill. Now please, just tell me what you want me to do and I'll do it. But don't fudge and then throw it up to me."

I didn't say anything for a moment. Then:

"Right. See you Monday afternoon."

"I love you, Bill."

"And I love you. Good night."

At the time, we both still meant it. I think.

Chapter
4

The next morning, I went back to Charlotte's for the tennis game. No one could have guessed anything had been wrong the night before, so marvelous was this remarkable woman's control over her emotions. She looked in fine shape when we met on her court, and we played two fast sets. Charlotte wasn't good, she was terrific. She beat me the first set, and I barely managed to win the second.

"Isn't Mother fantastic?" enthused Nicky, who had watched us as she played with a kitten.

"You know why she's so good? Because she's ruthless." And she made a Ruthless Tycoon face.

"Uh huh," said Charlotte as she tightened the braces on her racket. "And if I were as ruthless with you as I should be . . ."

"I know, I wouldn't be such a wise ass."

"Nicky—"

"Did you meet Zoltan?" she said to me, quickly, to cut off her mother. She held up the sealpoint kitten. "Zoltan's the reincarnation of Zoltan the Terrible, who ruled the Planet Fortran in the third century, B.C."

"Hello, Zoltan the Terrible," I said, tickling his ears. "Where's the Planet Fortran?"

"On Channel Nine," deadpanned Charlotte. "Just after the 'Star Trek' re-runs."

"Are you a Trekkie?" I asked Nicky.

"Are you kidding? 'Star Trek' is life."

"I met the actor once who played Mr. Spock."

She looked at me as if I had said I knew God.

"Really?" she whispered.

"Really. It was at a fund-raising party."

"You actually met him? You *touched* him?"

"Well, we shook hands."

She was so impressed, for once she was speechless. She just stared at me in silent awe.

But the silence didn't last long. As the three of us walked back to the rear terrace of the house, I noticed Nicky watching me out of the corner of her eye. It was almost as if she were studying me. Certainly, she *looked* studious. While her mother was putting her racket on a chair, Nicky took me aside and said, quietly, "I guess it was sort of a crazy idea of mine to want to meet you, but . . ." She squinted up at me, and I got the feeling she was trying to express something very genuine. "What I mean is, you're really awfully nice."

"For a politician?"

"No, I mean for a person. It would really be great if we could see you again."

Her mother joined us, putting her hand on her daughter's shoulder.

"The Congressman's a busy man." Maybe it was wishful thinking, but the way she said it made me think the mother, as well as the daughter, hated to say goodbye. So did the congressman. I was surprised how much I liked both of them. I stood there, not wanting to leave, trying desperately to think of something to say that was slightly above the totally banal. I failed. "Well, maybe we'll run into each other again. Thanks for the tennis."

I shook both their hands then, as they watched me, started back to Arnold's.

I felt oddly let down.

Arnold is a flying nut and owns a Beechcraft and a Piper Cub. Knowing I shared his enthusiasm if not his financial resources (I spent four years in the naval air force between college and law school), he had offered to let me use the Piper during the campaign if I paid for fuel, landing fees and so forth. I suppose accepting his offer was against the spirit, if not the letter, of fair campaign practices, but I'm no saint and the practical advantage of being able to get around the state quickly was too important for me to pass up. So I accepted, which explains how I could play tennis in East Hampton until ten and be at the Dorset Hotel in Manhattan by one. I went up to the small suite on the ninth floor that Tony Gleason had rented as our Manhattan campaign headquarters. And there was Tony, smoking his Cigarillos and in a foul mood, as I suspected he would be.

"You're late," was his warm greeting. "What held you up?"

"Tennis."

"Tennis in East Hampton. Wonderful. Why don't you work that into your speech this afternoon? They'll love it in Harlem."

Tony, who's fifty, is skinny, bald and has a face only his wife could love (and she does). He teethed on politics in Brooklyn and has spent the last twenty years of his life getting politicians elected. For getting out crowds, organization, press relations and the dozens of other details of running a campaign, there's no better man in the business, for which I respect him. He also knows every politician in the state, which means knowing who's paying off whom, who owes whom what debts and favors, and how to twist whose arm with what thinly veiled threat. Sound like blackmail, venery and corruption? Call it politics.

The side of politics I don't much like and try to keep clear of, but a side that's there. Tony was my resident expert. His tough-Irish cynicism rarely sees above the clay feet, but he knows the classic way to win elections. I wasn't in the race to lose, but I had some not-so-classic ideas about how to win, which had been the basis of more than one fight between us. As I took off my seersucker jacket I had the feeling we were about to have another.

"Here are some notes Herb made last night," he said, handing me a 3x5 card. Herb Ross was my young Harvard hotshot speechwriter. I prefer talking off the cuff, not liking set speeches, but I generally carry notes in my pocket for last-minute memory-joggers, and Herb feeds me the notes.

"Where is Herb?" I asked.

· "Getting the minibus. We're due at 110th Street at quarter to three. You've met Randy Bartholomew, haven't you?"

The Honorable Randolph A. Bartholomew was the black assemblyman who had agreed to introduce me.

"I know him."

"Randy told me he's not going to say much, but his being there will be a plus—and we need plusses."

I ignored the gibe.

"What time do we leave?" I asked.

"Quarter past two. That'll give us a half hour,

which is probably more than we need but what the hell. By the way, did I tell you you're an asshole to do this?"

I looked up.

"About ten times. But you know, Tony, I read in a comic book once that a senator is supposed to represent *all* the people of a state, not just the white, suburban, middle class with two point three children and a double garage."

"It's *image*, jocko. Your image is Mr. Clean from upstate who never gets mixed up with all the crap that goes on in the city. You're apple trees, Bill, not junkies. You go up to Harlem and suddenly people are going to start seeing hypodermic needles when they think of you."

"That's bullshit."

"It isn't! Besides, do you think those people up there are going to like you? Christ, you'll be lucky if they don't tie you to the tracks of the goddam A-train! You've got nothing to gain and everything to lose by going up there, so can you tell me why the hell you're doing it?"

I looked at him a moment.

"Because," I finally said, "I want to."

He groaned and muttered, "I wonder if Scoop Jackson's hiring on these days?"

It couldn't have been a worse day for politics. It was blisteringly hot and sweatily humid. As the Dalton-for-Senator minibus pulled into Harlem I saw naked kids racing through open hydrants and old people sitting on fire escapes. A sour Tony was driving while Herb Ross talked into the loud-speaker. "Come hear Congressman William Dalton at 110th Street and Amsterdam Avenue! Bill Dalton, a Democrat you'll be proud to call Senator! Three o'clock at 110th Street..."

The amplified message blared down hot streets, fighting the Rock and Reggae blasting from radios on window sills, invading the citizen's privacy and probably creating more hostility than interest. "A Democrat you'll be proud to call Senator" was our campaign slogan. I wondered what they were thinking. In politics, you have to believe in yourself if anyone else is going to believe in you. I believed in myself. I really believed I could do a better job representing these people than anyone else then on the political scene. At the time, no one else was coming to Harlem talking about welfare reform: blacks and welfare were political poison, and Tony wasn't the only one who had tried to talk me out of coming. On the other hand, how could anyone hoping to represent the people of New York in the Senate with any degree of honesty ignore the stupendous problems of the ghetto? I wasn't trying to set myself up as being particularly brave or noble, but I had to believe in myself and I couldn't believe in apple trees alone. I genuinely wanted these people to be proud to call me senator. But from the looks on their faces as they watched the minibus pass by, I knew it wasn't going to be easy.

We pulled up at Amsterdam and 110th be-

hind a black Mercedes. Campaign posters had
been put up and a crowd of about fifty was
gathered. I got out of the bus and a reeling wino
pointed at me and laughed. Randy Bartholomew
got out of his Mercedes and came over to shake
hands. He's a big, handsome man with gray hair,
a power in Harlem, and I don't particularly like
him. I've heard too many stories about how he
operates. Privately, I marveled at his nerve driving a thirteen thousand dollar car. On the other
hand, he probably figured it gave him a macho
success image. If he'd driven a Toyota, his constituents might have thought he was small time
or hypocritical or both.

Randy, Tony and I talked politics a moment.
It was all general, because Randy wasn't endorsing my candidacy; he was introducing me only
because he owed Tony a favor. Then he took the
mike and spoke to the crowd. "Folks," he said
(and for some reason, the "folks" business
amused me), "Bill Dalton's one of the best congressmen we've got in this state . . ."

"Who says?" interrupted a kid.

Randy glared at him majestically.

"*I* say."

The kid shut up.

"Now, he's from upstate," Randy continued.
"You know—*trees.* Ever hear of trees?" The
crowd hooted. Randy went on: "Anyway, upstate's
the enemy because upstate don't like to give New
York money, and we're big spenders—right?"

"You better believe it . . ."

"So if you treat Bill Dalton right, maybe he can loosen up those money bags in Albany and spread a little of the bread around. Got it? Let's give him a hand."

Perfunctory applause as he passed me the mike. It wasn't exactly the introduction of one's dreams, but I knew Randy wasn't going to talk about my senatorial ambitions. He wasn't going to say anything until the last-moment horsetrading began.

Holding the mike, I looked out at the black and brown faces. Young, old; housewives, passers-by; street types; one Borsalino-hatted, white-suited pimp; my friend, the wino. Then, to my surprise and shock, I saw at the edge of the crowd one very white face. Charlotte Dreyfus.

I almost blew my opening line.

"I want to talk about welfare . . ." I began.

"Ever been on it, Charlie?" called out a woman.

"No . . ."

"Then what you talkin' 'bout it for?"

"Because somebody's got to talk about it, and no one else is," I replied, which seemed to satisfy her for the moment. "As Assemblyman Bartholomew said, I'm from upstate, and I don't have to tell you that the people from my district, which is primarily rural, think welfare is—"

"A pile of shee-it!" offered a little girl, and everyone burst into laughter, including me.

"You gonna give me a job, honky?" yelled a man. "You give me a job and I'll get off welfare. How 'bout it, honky?"

"I can't give you a job," I answered, "and I'm not going to promise you that if you vote for me and I get elected senator I'll be able to get the government to give everyone a job. I'm going to tell it to you straight: the government isn't going to give everyone a job because it can't. What it *can* do—and what I think it *should* do—is guarantee everyone a minimum income—"

"You mean," yelled my first heckler, "you gonna give me money?"

"If you honestly can't get a job, if no government agency can find you work, then yes—I say give you money."

"This turkey am crazy!" yelled a man, and everyone laughed.

"What's the difference between that and welfare?" someone added.

"The difference is," I said, "that's *all* you get. You get a certain basic minimum income, but nothing else. No food stamps, no housing projects, no *nothing*. Because I can tell you from first-hand experience the money that's blown by the bureaucracy administering hundreds of different social programs—if that money were given out to *you* who are supposed to benefit by those programs . . . well, hell, who knows, maybe you could all own a Mercedes like Assemblyman Bartholomew . . ."

I turned to look at Bartholomew, who merely stared at me. (Tony Gleason looked ready to faint.) Now, there are few times in a politician's life when he coins a phrase that catches on, but I had just done it. Or rather, my lady heckler did it for me, because she yelled, "God-*damn!* A Mercedes in every pot!" And suddenly the whole crowd was laughing, clapping, cheering and whistling, and I realized I had a campaign slogan that just might make—or break—me. Probably the latter, because I quickly realized a line like that could cause me a lot of trouble later on. But at least at the moment I had obviously caught the imagination of the crowd. The people who had been so hostile a moment before were suddenly for me. It was a heady experience, but I at least had the sense to quit while I was ahead. I held up my hand and said, "That's my program, ladies and gentlemen. A minimum income for everyone, and no government programs that put the money into the politician's pockets instead of yours. And I believe I can sell this idea to my constituents upstate because I can *prove* to them that in the long run it's going to cost them less. Anyway, thanks for listening to me, and I hope like hell it cools off."

Applause and cheers. Grinning, I handed the mike to Tony (who looked shell-shocked), then walked into the crowd, pressing the flesh and talking to people individually. I was surprised how new the idea was to them—after all, it had been kicking around for years. But no one apparently had ever taken the trouble to come up

and talk to these people about it face to face.
They immediately saw the advantages. "Man, that
would mean no more welfare cheats, wouldn't it?"
said one young man, pumping my hand. "It
should cut a lot of it out," I answered. "I could
buy my own food with my own money and not
use those damned food stamps, couldn't I?" said
one white-haired woman who must have been
eighty. I told her that was the whole idea—to
give people the dignity of allocating their money
their *own* way. But first society has to admit that
a rich country like ours has the obligation to
guarantee everyone a basic income—and to
realize that it makes better sense economically,
and will cost far less, than the present gargan-
tuan, cumbersome and inefficient system.

By the time I reached Charlotte my hand was
sore from shaking, and I was dripping sweat. But
I was still grinning. She was too.

"You really are some kind of nut," she said.
"No wonder Nicky flipped over you."

"Thanks. And what are you doing here?"

"I wanted to see if you're for real. I liked what
I heard. Do you think it can work?"

"I know it can work, if someone could get
those lunkheads in Washington to give it a
chance."

"Well, I'm willing to bet a thousand *you* can
get them to give it a chance."

Just then I spotted Tony Gleason heading for
me around the edge of the crowd, and I grabbed
Charlotte's arm.

"Come on, let's get out of here," I said, hustling her toward a cab.

"Where are we going?"

"My campaign manager's going to scream bloody murder at me for the Mercedes line, and I'm too hot to listen to him. So I'm buying you a drink in an air-conditioned bar."

"Would you settle for my apartment?"

"You're on."

And we climbed into the cab. As it pulled away, I looked through the rear window to see Tony mouthing "You son of a bitch" at me.

I felt wonderful.

I eased back in the seat and looked at her.

"Hey, it's great to see you," I said. "How'd you get here?"

"I chartered a plane."

"Why didn't you tell me? I could have brought you in with me."

She hesitated.

"Well, something came up after you left, and I had to get Nicky back to town in a hurry. And then I remembered your speech, so I thought I'd drop by and see you in action. You're pretty good, you know. Really."

It was the second hint I had that something was wrong.

"Why did you have to get back in a hurry?"

Again she hesitated, as if weighing whether to tell me. She decided against it.

"Oh, it's some trouble she's been having."

"It must be serious if you had to charter a plane—"

Her face was a mask.

"It was only a toothache . . . didn't your campaign manager know what you were going to say?"

"*I* didn't know! 'A Mercedes in every pot'—what a line! I wonder if I have the nerve to use it?"

"Isn't it a bit misleading?"

"I know, but the *idea* is a good one. Well, at least it should shake some people up. The trouble with this country is, the politicians are all carbon copies of each other. I may end up out of a job, but at least I won't be a carbon copy."

"I don't think you're going to end up out of a job."

I liked the way she said that.

The cab pulled up in front of one of those twenties co-op buildings on Fifth Avenue that are bastions of old money, and an attendant opened the door and handed us out of the cab.

"Good afternoon, Miss Dreyfus," he said, touching the bill of his cap.

"Good afternoon, Pete."

I followed Charlotte into the dark green marble lobby, which was blissfully cool.

"This is certainly a change from 110th Street," I muttered, looking around.

"Want to go someplace else?"

"No."

We entered the paneled elevator, and a white-haired retainer stepped in to push the button marked PH.

"Bill, this is Charlie Simmons," said Charlotte. "Charlie, meet Congressman Bill Dalton whose going to be our next senator."

"Maybe," I said, shaking Charlie's hand.

"Glad to meet you, congressman."

"How's the knee, Charlie?" continued Charlotte. "Charlie sprained his knee last week bowling."

"Not bad today, Miss Dreyfus. I used your heating pad, like you said, and it really helped."

"That's a fabulous heating pad. My mother bought it back in the thirties, and they just don't make heating pads the same any more, don't ask me why."

"They don't make anything the same any more, Miss Dreyfus."

"Amen to that."

The elevator stopped, the doors slid open and we entered Wonderland.

"This is one of the great New York apartments," Charlotte said matter-of-factly as she led me into the weird foyer. "Mother bought it in the twenties after she hit it big, I grew up in it and I love it. It's the three top floors of the building. Isn't that wild? Can you believe this foyer?"

Actually it was difficult to believe. It was a big square room, the floor and walls of which were black marble. Around the walls, inlaid in the marble, marched bronze Egyptian figures in bas relief, their bodies head-on, their faces and feet in profile. From the white vaulted ceiling hung a bronze chandelier shaped like a Sphinx.

"Mother was in her Egyptian Period when she put this in," Charlotte said, taking her key from her purse, "and I haven't the heart to change it. I call it Ramses Camp. I had a cocktail party for the U.J.A. here last year, and they about fainted."

"Can I ask a dumb question?"

"Sure."

"Why do you need an elevator man when you have an automatic elevator?"

She fit the key into the lock of the bronze door.

"Two years ago Charlie retired and we put in the automatic elevators. Then we found we missed him so much, we bribed him to un-retire. The nice thing was, he said he missed us too . . . Well, welcome to my pad."

She pushed the bronze door open and we entered yet another foyer. This one was round and had a graceful circular stairway coiling up to the second floor and, beyond, the third. At the top was one of those wonderful round skylights they made in the old days, the leading of which formed a graceful spider's web and through the center of which plunged a long chain that dropped down through the stairwell, terminating in a handsome lantern. The floor was white and black marble, and beneath the stair was an elevator.

"You have your own elevator?" I asked wonderingly.

"That's right. Decadent, isn't it?"

She clicked across the marble to a long hallway lined with prints and paintings, some jazzily modern, others handsomely old. As I followed her down the hall past closed doors she said, "My mother was interested in art and she bought some pretty daring stuff for her day, although she was basically conservative. I bought a lot of Pop-art stuff but I'm getting tired of it, except for Oldenburg, who makes me laugh. Do you like him?"

"I'm afraid I'm a little out of it when it comes to modern art."

She stopped in front of a large framed print. It was a sketch of a gigantic wall plug standing in Central Park.

"That's Oldenburg," she said.

I looked at the wall plug a moment.

"It's a plug, isn't it?" I asked, with no little confusion.

"That's right."

I looked at it again, not quite certain I got the "message." She watched me. Then I looked at her and shrugged.

"It's a plug," I said, giving up. We both laughed and continued down the hall. Finally we emerged into a living room like one of those living rooms they used to have in Hollywood movies about the New York rich. It was about forty-five feet long, filled with antiques, and had two crystal chandeliers. The tables were jammed with bibelots, the black Steinway grand was loaded with silver-framed photos of celebrities past and present, all autographed, the walls were covered with art and between two of the French doors leading out to the terrace was a large statue of a Chinese goddess, one of the most beautiful things I'd ever seen.

"That's a Ch'ien Lung Kuan Yin," she said, pointing to the statue. "Kuan Yin was the Chinese Goddess of Luck, so you'd better be nice to her if you want to be senator. Clyde's driving the car in from the Island, so I'll bartend. What would you like?"

"Something cool. White wine?"

"Fine. Go on out to the terrace and enjoy the view. I'll be with you in a minute."

I walked out onto the terrace, which wrapped around three sides of the penthouse. The terrace was wide, tiled and an enchanted garden. Trees, shrubs, flowers, ivies were everywhere. A handsome iron satyr's-head spat water from the wall into a cast-iron basin filled with lilies. White chaises and chairs were scattered about, with glass-top tables here and there. I took it all in, then went to the waist-high brick wall and looked out over Central Park. The sun, arching overhead toward the Russian-Gothic towers of Central Park West, beat down, baking the city, which shimmered in the heat. It was a magnificent view and I was hardly immune to its beauties. But far to the north lay Harlem, where fifteen minutes before I had been in such a vastly different neighborhood. I didn't exactly blame Charlotte for living in such queenly splendor, nor did I resent it. But I couldn't help feeling a little uncomfortable.

"Are you going to have an affair with Mother?"

I turned to see Nicky twirling toward me. She had on a black leotard and looked as though she had been doing ballet exercises. She stopped in front of me, went "Ta ta!" and did a low curtsy. "Aren't I sen-*say*-tional?"

"How many times do I have to tell you?"

"I need constant reassurance because I'm basically insecure."

"You're about as insecure as Muhammad Ali. I thought you had a toothache?"

She looked at me curiously, then shrugged.

"Oh, *that*. It got fixed—sort of. But I *am* insecure. I'm going to be the Margot Fonteyn of 1980 if I can overcome my insecurity. I'll dance before all the crowned heads of Europe and have four hundred and thirty-two lovers, including Muhammad Ali and Joe Namath. You didn't answer my question."

"No, I'm not going to have an affair with your mother."

"Why not? She's beautiful."

I crossed my arms and tried hard to look stern.

"In the first place, my sex life is none of

your business. In the second place, I love my wife and wouldn't cheat on her."

She cocked her head slightly and looked at me.

"You're weird," she finally said. "Everybody cheats on their wives. Even my shrink does."

"You have a psychiatrist?"

"Of course. Doesn't everyone?"

"But you're only eleven!"

"I'm almost twelve, and what's that got to do with it? There's a teenage sexplosion— haven't you heard? Not that I've exploded yet ... but I think about it a lot. Dr. Kornbloom's sex life is much more interesting than mine. He's my shrink, and he's having an affair with his nurse Sylvia, who's a real sexpot. He tells me all about his guilt feelings. He's miserable but he can't help himself. I *really* wish you'd have an affair with mother."

"Why?"

"Because ... then you'd be around a lot."

She looked at me rather wistfully, and suddenly she seemed very much her own age, and I felt a rush of affection for her. Maybe it was simplistic psychology on my part, but I had the feeling she was beginning to look on me as a potential father-substitute.

I smiled at her and said, "Well, maybe I can be around some anyway."

She brightened. "Would you? Really? That would be super!" At which point she went up *en pointe* and began fluttering about. I watched her with admiration. After a moment I asked, "Where do you study ballet?"

She stopped dancing and flopped in a chair. "I have a private instructor named Signor Bellini. He's wonderful."

"Where do you go to school?"

"The Brearley. We start after Labor Day. I'm a problem pupil. The teachers would all like to garrote me. Do you believe in child torture?"

"*I* do," said her mother, coming out on the terrace with two wineglasses. "And who let Queen Kong out of her cage?"

Nicky leapt out of her chair and went into a gorilla act, stooping over and swinging her arms as she shuffled around the terrace. "Me Kong," she grunted. "Me look for tiny white maiden to make love to. Me carry her to top of Empire State Building and make like big phallic symbol—"

"You make like Super-Brat, as usual," said Charlotte. "Let's scratch this number. You need a new act or a new agent. Besides, Bill needs peace and quiet."

Nicky looked at me excitedly.

"How was your speech? Were you a sensation?"

"He was," said Charlotte, sitting under the green-striped awning which was half unrolled.

"Tell me what you said! I want to hear the whole speech!"

"Nicky, *please*. It's hot. Now leave us alone."

She looked at the two of us rather conspira-

torially, then started toward the door. "All
right," she said. "Good-by, Bill. When will I see
you again?"

"I'll be back in town Tuesday."

She paused by the door to the living room,
giving us a sultry, suggestive look.

"I'll leave you two *alone*," she said, leaning
heavily on the "alone." Then she was gone.

I sat down next to Charlotte. "Something
tells me she wants a man around the house."

"She's not exactly subtle, is she? She misses
a father, which I feel guilty about."

"You never re-married?"

"Oh yes, two years ago. A Wall Street type
—Yale, old family, very solid. I thought after my
first disaster he'd be perfect."

"And?"

"Wrong again. One night about a year after
we'd married I came back to the apartment to
find a note on my bed. He'd taken off with my
best friend. It turned out they'd been an item
for six months. So much for solid Yalies."

"Not to mention Wall Street. Was Nicky upset?"

"No. She never liked him much. I was never
sure why, except maybe she saw how flakey he
was underneath. I sometimes think she's a better
judge of character than I am."

"And now? No prospective number three on
the horizon?"

"No, and I'm just as glad. Except for Nicky,
of course. After two disasters I'm beginning to

wonder if it isn't my fault. Maybe I'm just not good wife material. I'm independent, I have my business . . ." She shrugged, then added, "On the other hand, it can get pretty lonely. . . ."

I won't pretend that the idea of making love to Charlotte Dreyfus hadn't entered my head long before Nicky brought it up. Charlotte was a beautiful woman, a smart woman and last but hardly least, a sexy woman. I liked her more each time I saw her. It wasn't only that she seemed to like me as well and was enthusiastic about my speech—though that helped, creatures of ego that we all are. There was also a mystery about her that intrigued me, a kind of sadness in her gray eyes—just as at that moment—that made this apparently self-sufficient woman seem vulnerable and, to me, that much more desirable. She was looking so desirable, in fact, that warning signals were flashing in my mind. For even in this increasingly casual age, involvements are something politicians think twice about (which isn't to say plenty don't go right ahead anyway). But more than that, what I had told Nicky was true: I did love Peggy. In eighteen years I had never cheated on her. Not that there hadn't been opportunities and temptations. In Washington, for a congressman on the green side of ninety . . . well, you read the papers. Anyway, call me square, but I respected my wife and my family.

Still, warning lights were flashing. Charlotte must have sensed it too, because she abruptly changed the subject.

"You say you'll be back in town Tuesday?"

"Yes. I've got to go back to West Schuyler tomorrow. A local TV station is taping an interview with me and Peggy in our house. One of those see-the-candidate-at-home numbers. If it turns out well, maybe we'll use it to show around the state. The voters aren't going to see too much of Peggy in the flesh."

"I've seen a picture of her. She's very attractive."

"Yes, she is."

Silence. I forced myself to look at my watch.

"Well, the coach is turning into a pumpkin. Thanks for the drink, but I've got a staff meeting at four-thirty." I finished my wine and stood up. She got up also and took two pieces of paper from the pocket of her dress.

"These are for you," she said.

I took them. One was a check for a thousand dollars, made out to my campaign. The other was a scrap of paper with an address in the East Eighties written on it.

"I know what this is," I said, putting the check in my wallet. "And I thank you for it. But what's the address?"

"A place I'd very much like you to meet me at Tuesday afternoon, if you've got some free time."

"Sounds mysterious."

She smiled.

"Is there a law saying a woman can't be mysterious? Could you make it about five?"

I had two days full of appointments, which was why I was coming back to the city. But I did happen to be free later that afternoon.

"You've got a date. I hope it's a den of iniquity?"

"Definitely," she said, leading me back into the apartment.

Chapter 5

The staff meeting was an excuse. I was beginning to feel guilty about Tony, and I thought I'd better get back to the hotel and placate him. When I came into the room, he and Herb stared at me.

"Greetings," I said cheerily, closing the door and diving into the fog of Cigarillo smoke that the air conditioner was recirculating with gagging efficiency. "How'd you like the speech?"

"Oh, it was memorable," said Tony. "'A Mercedes in every pot' has real poetry to it. How about 'A dead candidate in every newspaper'? Or, better yet: 'Dalton Wants to Redistribute the

Wealth.' Mm, I like that. That's got the *real* kiss of death to it. Why don't you just proposition a nun and get it over with?"

"Dalton doesn't want to redistribute the wealth," I said, taking a Tab from the small icebox. "But Dalton's fed up with the welfare mess and Dalton wants a little drama in his campaign. You got drama, didn't you?"

"Oh, we got drama. Look, Bill, aside from the fact that you've made a blood enemy of Randy Bartholomew ..."

"Why? Because I mentioned he owns a Mercedes?"

"Jesus, things like that you don't mention!"

"Hell, it was sitting there, wasn't it? Those people have eyes! I didn't say anything they didn't know, did I?"

"But you don't *mention* it!" he yelled in exasperation. Then he simmered down. "Okay, look: it's your campaign. Herb and I are only your advisors, right? We do what you want. If you want me to kill the story, I think I can still do it. If you want my advice, I'd kill it. It's not going to look good. I don't have to remind you that all it took were a couple of tears out of Muskie's eyes in New Hampshire to blow his chances for the nomination in '72—and that was for the Presidency, yet. One Mercedes in every pot out of your big mouth can easily blow the Senate nomination, believe me. So: do I try to kill it?"

I gulped down half the Tab, eyeing Tony and Herb.

"No," I said. "Let them print it. The *idea's* a good one, and I'll defend it. I want to."

Tony shrugged helplessly.

"Why aren't I in aluminum siding? Aluminum siding is safe . . . it pays well . . . why aren't I in aluminum siding?"

I laughed. "Because you're a whore for politics."

"You're right," he sighed. "Goddammit, you're right. By the way, who was the dame you hustled into the cab?"

I took out Charlotte's check from my wallet and gave it to him. "That was Charlotte Dreyfus, president and major stockholder of Marguerite Dreyfus Cosmetics, Inc. She also is a believer in your candidate."

He looked at the check, then looked at me, his vote-tabulator eyes clicking with suspicion.

"And . . . ?"

"Don't start overworking that imagination of yours, Tony. Charlotte Dreyfus is a friend. Period."

He didn't say anything as he folded the check and stuffed it into his shirt pocket. He didn't have to. The look on his face said it all.

To my relief, the Monday morning papers gave a generally favorable coverage to my speech. The *Times* even ran a short editorial entitled "A Mercedes in Every Pot" in which they took me to task for "irresponsible phrasemaking"— though I actually hadn't made it up—but praised me for "resurrecting an idea that Washington had prematurely buried" and "opening a dialogue on a subject of paramount importance to the city, the state and the nation." By nine o'clock I had gotten calls from two TV stations asking for interviews, which I agreed to; by noon, when I left for La Guardia to get my plane for the trip home, the interviews had been taped and I thought I had come across pretty well. And by the time I landed at the small airport outside West Schuyler, I was really feeling good. An issue I thought was important was attracting attention. My campaign was taking off.

I keep my four-year-old Ford at the airport, so I drove into town, then out the other side where, in a mid-sixties development named (unfortunately) River Glen, our pleasant split-level mid-sixties development house is located not far from the Erie Canal (the "River" in River Glen is really the canal, but presumably the developer thought "Canal Glen" lacked sales appeal). A TV truck was parked in the driveway but Peggy's car wasn't, which surprised me. Jeff was shooting baskets. I asked him where his mother was.

"She left about a half hour ago to show somebody a house," he said.

I looked at my watch. It was twenty past two.

"Does she know they want to tape at three?"

"She said she'd be back in time."

I went quickly into the house, where a three-man crew was setting up the lights and the camera in our living room. The interviewer was Julia Ridley, who is known as Utica's answer to Barbara Walters (I was never sure what the question was). I talked to Julia a few minutes and then, since there was still no sign of Peggy, I went into the kitchen to call her office.

In 1970 a developer had bought a farm not far from town and announced plans to put up a shopping center. The farm had once been in Peggy's family, she had spent summers on it when she was a kid and she had a natural affection for it that turned to outrage when she heard what was being planned for it. Peggy was always energetic, and now she channeled her energies into saving that farm. She organized a committee, besieged the town's zoning board, and made the developer out to be such an unmitigated villain that he made a hasty retreat and put the farm back on the market. To prevent him from changing his mind, Peggy beat the bushes for a buyer. Successful again, the farm saved, Peggy felt justifiably triumphant. A byproduct of the whole experience was that she became so interested in real estate she went into the business herself (*not* as a developer, I might add). She got her license, opened a small office, and discovered she was not only good at selling houses, she loved it; her first year she cleared over $15,000, which in a small community like West Schuyler is damned good money. I was glad Peggy had found a career she enjoyed (and frankly not unhappy about a second income helping the family finances), except of course her business made her even more reluctant to leave West Schuyler for Washington and even less enchanted with her role as the wife of Congressman Dalton. As I said, her growing invisibility in that role was becoming somewhat awkward, politically. And taking off to show a house minutes before a scheduled TV show was, I thought, just a bit gratuitous.

Her secretary said she hadn't heard from her, but she knew the place she was showing and gave me the address. Telling Julia Ridley I'd be back soon, I drove across town to Woodlawn Avenue, where I hoped to find my industrious wife. In fact, her Pontiac was parked in front of the house. So was a tow truck. I parked, got out and came up to Peggy, who was watching Sid Parson, a local mechanic, fiddle with the engine.

"The car went dead," she said as I kissed her. "Sid says it's the alternator or something. What's an alternator?"

I was in no mood to explain.

"You know, the TV people are in the house..."

"I know, but there's plenty of time."

"Fifteen minutes."

Sid assured us he'd bring the car around when he'd fixed it (one of the advantages of small towns), so Peggy got into my car and we started back to the house. We drove in silence for a while, though I knew she was watching me.

"You're angry," she finally said.

"A little."

"I would have gotten there in time. Sid would have brought me."

"You also might have called, or left a message at your office. Or something."

"Bill, I was *trying* to get the car started! I thought it was more important to get Sid there than leave messages all over town. I *am* a responsible person—you know that—and I certainly wouldn't have left you holding the bag."

"All right, let's forget it."

Nothing more was said; but fifteen minutes later, when the candidate and his wife sat on their living room sofa and smiled into the camera, a viewer might have been justified in thinking the candidate's smile just a bit forced. Evidently Julia Ridley thought so, because she quickly brought the conversation around to political marriages. "Is it difficult being a politician's wife, Mrs. Dalton?" she asked.

Charlotte had described Peggy as "attractive," and she is. She dresses well, has a good figure, is smart, poised and a good straightforward interviewee. Under the circumstances, I was interested in her answer.

"Frankly," she said, "it's not easy. Particularly when you have other interests, as I do."

"Is that why you haven't taken too active a role in your husband's campaigns?"

Peggy smiled.

"But I *have*," she corrected. "And I am now. I mean, I'm on this program, for example. But

I'll also say that I think politicians' families have gotten too much into campaigns lately. After all, people are voting for the candidate, not his or her family. The voters should be interested in the candidate and the issues."

"But," said Julia, "isn't a person's character reflected by his family to a certain extent? And isn't a politician's character as important as the issues? In fact, it's *become* an issue."

It was a God-sent opportunity for me.

"I agree," I said, then turned to Peggy. "See? You're going to have to do more campaigning, Peg."

It was casual and friendly, but I suppose I also knew Peggy would feel she was being needled in public.

There was an awkward pause, and Julia, sensing tension, led us further into dangerous waters. "Do you think" she said, with her saccharine smile, "that political marriages have more pressures on them than other marriages?"

"Yes," said Peggy.

"Recently there's been a rash of politicians going through divorces and a good deal of publicity about politicians' private lives. Do you think a politician should *not* try to save a bad marriage for the sake of his public image?"

This, to me. I thought a moment before answering. "Well, voters are pretty sophisticated these days. I mean, with the divorce rate so high in the country, most people aren't too quick to judge others harshly when it comes to a divorce.

On the other hand, let me say that I think we Americans are getting too casual about divorces. I think we tend to forget that a successful marriage takes effort on both sides. Divorce can too often be the lazy way out."

Love is a fairly shopworn word in our society, and I suppose we all have at best only a vague idea of what it means. As I look back, I don't think I was really aware of being in love with Charlotte at the time. If I had been, I certainly would never have made those throbbing public pronounciamentos. Certainly, in light of what happened, I was exposing myself to the charge of the rankest hypocrisy and double-talk.

Still, if I weren't consciously in love with her, Charlotte was very much in my mind, and I was definitely looking forward to seeing her again the next Tuesday. I suppose that should have tipped me off. At least enough to have kept my big mouth shut.

Chapter
6

In retrospect, I suppose I should have guessed something was seriously wrong with Nicky. Bringing her back to New York in a chartered plane, the "toothache" business, Charlotte's odd "moods," Nicky's strange look when I asked her how her tooth was—I should have guessed. Except, an eleven-year-old brimming with vitality? Well, that Tuesday I found out.

The mysterious Upper East Side address Charlotte had given me turned out to be a nondescript brownstone in the middle of a block that had seen better days. It was raining, and as I climbed the steps I wondered what dark mystery she was about to reveal to me. There was a small brass plaque next to the door that said "Dreyfus House," which wasn't particularly enlightening.

Charlotte was waiting for me in the center hall, and though she smiled as she shook my hand, I got the impression that she was decidedly nervous about something. I remember thinking that she seemed, well, haunted—which should have been another clue. Except it didn't register.

"What's Dreyfus House?" I asked, looking around.

"Come on, and I'll show you."

She led me down the hall, the walls of which had been splashed with colorful murals of New York street scenes.

"This used to be a boarding house," she said. "About five years ago we bought it and refurbished it. Most of the rooms are studios now. These murals were done by the kids."

"What kids?"

"Kids from the barrio who are sent to us by referral agencies. Kids who are interested in art and have talent. We give them free instruction, studio space, materials—then if they're good enough we give them scholarships to art school. We've got thirty-five scholarships in effect right now."

We had reached the end of the hall. She opened two doors and led me into a big room at the back of the house. Here the walls were pure white, and new modern windows had replaced smaller predecessors to admit light. In the middle of the room, sitting on a stool on a small platform, was a nude model. Around her, working at sketch pads on easels, were about a dozen young people of both sexes. Charlotte whispered to me, "This used to be the kitchen and dining room. We converted them into a lecture hall and workroom."

We watched for a few minutes, then Charlotte led me to a young Puerto Rican whom she introduced as Juan Morales. "Juanito," as she called him, was about sixteen, strikingly handsome and, judging from his charcoal sketch of the model, talented. "Juanito's the Freddie Prinze of the art world," said Charlotte. "He's so good he scares me." They chatted for a few minutes as I noted the nude model. Finally I casually asked, "Who's the model?"

"My sister," said Juanito matter-of-factly.

For some reason that threw me. Charlotte suppressed a laugh as she took me to the second floor where, in a back room, was her own studio. It was a small room overlooking the garden with workbenches built around the walls. The place was a mess, strewn with mallets, woodworking tools, welding equipment, rags. A large sculpture stood in the middle of the room. It's not easy to describe, but basically it consisted of three pieces of iron forming a teepee-type tripod, at the top of which unfinished wood boards exploded in various directions.

"This is what I'm working on now," she said. "You like?"

My mind raced to find an appropriately non-committal reply.

"Well, it's . . ."

"Interesting?" she suggested drily.

"Oh, it's certainly that."

She burst into laughter.

"Oh God, you're wonderful! Why don't you admit you think it's awful?"

"Because I don't. As I told you, I don't . . . I mean, I'm not exactly an expert on modern art. How often do you come here?"

"As often as I can. I love sculpting. That was what I wanted to be first, you know. It was part of my big rebellion."

"Against your mother?"

"Yes, I adored her, but she was *so* successful, *so* glamorous, I felt like the Ugly Duckling around her."

"*You?*"

"I was a mess till I was about twenty. Braces on my teeth, stringy hair, the works. Boys looked at me and turned to stone. Anyway, I wanted to show Mother I could do something on my own. So I went to the Village and started sculpting. I wanted to sculpt more than anything in the world."

"What went wrong?"

"It turned out I didn't have any talent. Maybe that's why I'm so indulgent with Nicky.

She *does* have talent, she wants to be a ballerina and I suppose in a way I've been living vicariously through her. See? I'm the classic stage mother."

"But you *have* made it."

"In business? Yes, but that's second best. A good second best but still . . ."

I looked at the sculpture again.

"Those kids downstairs," I said, "they really like you."

"Yes, I think so. They didn't at first. I had to earn their respect. But I don't like them until they earn *my* respect. I may be a limousine liberal but I'm no sucker."

"So the 'we' of this place is you?"

"Yes."

"And why did you want me to see it?"

"Because the other day when you were at the apartment I had the feeling you were thinking, 'this woman has too damned much.' Maybe I'm needlessly defensive but I wanted you to see that I *do* do things with my money besides going to charity balls. Do you mind?"

"That you brought me here? Why should I mind? I'm impressed."

She looked troubled.

"Well, to be honest, I wanted to impress you. There's something I want to ask you to do for me . . . Actually, it's for Nicky . . . I don't suppose you're free for dinner tonight?"

"I'm sitting on a panel discussion at the New School on 'The Coming Crisis in Social Security.'

If you can wait until after Social Security has
had its crisis, I'm all yours."

"Then you can be at the apartment at eight-
thirty?"

The panel discussion at the New School ran
overtime, so I didn't arrive at the apartment until close to nine. Clyde let me in and told me Miss
Dreyfus was in the living room. I walked through
the circular foyer, then down the long art-lined
corridor, wondering why the apartment seemed
so quiet. Perhaps it was the lugubrious effect of
the Egyptian foyer, which at night seemed murk-
ily tomblike; perhaps it was the fact that sixteen
floors above Fifth Avenue one suddenly missed
the street noises of Greenwich Village. Whatever
it was, I felt I was walking on black velvet.

And then I reached the living room and was
greeted by a spectacular sight: Charlotte was
standing next to the statue of Kuan Yin, looking
out over the terrace to the city below. Now she
turned and looked at me. She was wearing a
black dinner dress that was so simple it looked
. . . I suppose "slinky" is the word, though that
implies a vulgarity that wasn't there. It just
showed off her splendid body. There were spa-
ghetti straps over her bare shoulders, and her
arms seemed less tan in the soft night light. She
was wearing a large ruby and diamond ring, and
there were ruby and diamond clips on her dress.
She looked like Sargent's Madame X, or perhaps
Carole Lombard, or perhaps a little of both.

"How was the coming crisis of Social Security?" she asked.

"On its way. Sorry I'm late, but they were asking a lot of questions."

"Shall we eat now, or do you want a drink first?"

"Let's eat. I'm starved."

I followed her to the end of the room, where she opened two doors and led me into the dining room. By now I was growing accustomed to the lavish beauty of the place, but the dining room was yet another stunner. The walls were covered with what I guessed was an antique Chinese wallpaper: delicate pagodas and graceful figures against a pale yellow background. A crystal chandelier hung from the tall ceiling over the wood table, which gleamed with vermeil candlesticks and flatware. A China bowl was filled with chrysanthemums and daisies. In the corner, masking the kitchen door, was a tall Chinese screen that matched the wallpaper. Over the sideboard hung a Boudin seascape, and across the room from it two charming Pissarro girls smiled at each other. I don't know whether it was the gold on the table, the crystal, the undoubtedly expensive paints, the rubies and diamonds—or, more likely, all of it put together—which got to me, but unthinkingly I muttered, "God, you're so damn rich it scares me."

It was the wrong thing to say. She turned on me and snapped, "Well, what the hell am I supposed to do, eat off Tupperware?"

"No, but—"

"But what? I'm *not* going to have my life style thrown up in my face! I've *earned* it. I also do a lot of good with my money and—"

I raised my hands. "Don't shoot. I give up."

She cooled down. "I'm sorry. It's just that my mother always said, 'If there's anything more vulgar than a poor woman trying to look rich, it's a rich woman trying to look poor.' Maybe she was rationalizing *her* life style, but I think she was right."

I held the chair for her, and she sat down. I sat at the side of the table next to her.

"I really *am* sorry," she said, taking a deep breath. "I'm afraid I'm in a rotten mood ... You see, Nicky's been in the hospital again."

I looked at her rather dumbly.

"What's wrong with her?"

"She's dying." She said it looking straight ahead.

"*Nicky?*"

She nodded.

"I found out for certain last week. She has acute lymphatic leukemia. The doctors say she has about six weeks to live."

At which point Clyde brought in the first course, for which I was grateful because I was too numb to think of anything to say to her. The idea of that vital child having her life so abruptly and prematurely terminated almost literally nauseated me. Charlotte was watching me. After Clyde left the room she said, "I didn't want to tell you, but that's why I had to bring her back to town Sunday. She had to have another transfusion. And then, this afternoon we had to take her back for another . . ." She closed her eyes a moment, whether from weariness or despair I couldn't tell. Probably both. Then she opened them. "That was why . . . you know . . . the other night out at East Hampton when she put on her Zombie act, I got sick. I'd just found out two days before, and I guess I was still in shock . . . and then all her crazy talk about graves . . ." She stopped, then added, softly, "I wish it *were* a toothache."

"There's nothing they can *do?*" I said, realizing now why the apartment had seemed so strangely quiet.

"No. They say if she had ordinary leukemia she'd have a fairly good chance—they *can* cure that in some cases. But not what she's got. There's no chemotherapy, there's nothing. I tell myself a miracle might happen . . ."

"Does she know?"

"I don't think so. At least I haven't told her." She toyed with her wineglass a moment, then: "Do you think I should?"

"Oh my God, I don't know. If she were older . . ."

"If she were older, yes, I'd tell her. I think a person has the right to know. But she's so young . . ."

"She certainly must know something's wrong."

"Oh yes. She kept getting tired, and I took her in for tests. We've told her she has a type of anemia." She hesitated, then added, "It's possible she's guessed."

It all seemed so impersonal, the way we were discussing it, and yet how else does one discuss something so monstrous as the impending death of a child? I still wasn't really believing it. Something like that takes time to comprehend. Time. Six weeks, Charlotte had said. Now that I look back on it, I think that's what kept going through my mind. Six weeks. In the normal course of a life she should have had four thousand weeks, but she was only getting six. Charlotte was obviously thinking the same thing as she said, "Rotten, isn't it? Of *all* people to have it happen to."

Without thinking I reached over and squeezed her hand. I didn't know what else to do. Or to say. What *can* you say?

She forced a smile. "She's nuts about you, you know. And I realize it's wrong for me to drag you into my problems but—"

"I don't mind being dragged in."

"Then can I ask you another favor?"

"Try me."

"Do you think you could maybe find some time to take her out? To a movie or something? Maybe just a walk in the park. It would be fantastic for her. The hospital really bugged her . . . and I'm afraid there's only so much I can really do for her. She wants a father."

And of course, her own was dead. My schedule was packed with politics, but helping Nicky was more important.

"Of course I'll take her out," I said. "I'd be glad to."

We looked at each other a moment. Then she said, "You know, I've never felt totally helpless before. It's not a good feeling."

I knew what she meant. I felt the same way.

We didn't talk about Nicky during the rest of the meal, but she was very much in my mind. I suspect I'm as afraid of death as most people and, like most people, I think about it as little as possible. But now death was in the house and it was impossible to ignore. I wondered at how blind I'd been to what was really going through Charlotte's head and what the situation really was; but in my defense, she had been careful to hide what was happening, and had gone out of her way to act "normal" with her daughter. I told myself I would have to do the same. Nicky would immediately spot any change in my attitude, any softness or—God forbid—involuntary show of pity. I would have to be as tough as Charlotte. I didn't think it was going to be easy.

After coffee we went upstairs to the second floor, where Charlotte knocked on Nicky's door. In a moment the door was opened and I was jolted by her appearance of vitality and health. She was wearing her black leotards again and had pulled over them a T-shirt with the bearded face of Tchaikovsky stenciled on it. Her face lit up as she saw us.

"Invasion of the Adult Monsters!" she exclaimed, coming into the hall and closing the door behind her. "The Child Ghetto is off-limits to Adult Monsters."

"Uh-huh. Is that the TV I heard?" said Charlotte.

"Of course. It's the Sacred Hour."

" 'Star Trek'? Haven't you seen all those about ten times?"

"Yes, but this is one of my favorites. Mr. Spock's mind is taken over by the Ruler of the Crab Nebula and the Enterprise is almost swallowed up by a black hole. It's super. How are you, Bill? Are you going to spend the night?"

"Cool it," said Charlotte. "Listen, Child Monster, by some improbable twist of fate this mush-headed congressman has taken a fancy to you and wants to make a date."

Nicky looked at me and gasped, "It's love! I knew we were fated to have a burning romance the moment our hungry eyes met! Can Nicky Dreyfus Find Happiness with an Older Man? Or Is This Love Doomed? Can They Overcome the Prejudice of a Bigoted Society or—"

"*Nicky.*"

"Sorry. Where are you taking me?"

"Where do you want to go?" I asked.

"To lunch! A romantic lunch in some horribly overpriced French restaurant! And we can make love with our eyes."

"Well, I'm nearsighted, but lunch sounds great. Shall I pick you up at noon?"

"Oh, I couldn't possibly be ready by noon. In the first place, I'm having breakfast in bed with Henry Kissinger. Then at ten Joe Namath and I are working out at his private fur-lined gym . . ."

"Then maybe we'd better skip it?"

"I'll be *ready!* At noon—I'll be ready! Don't you dare not show! Mother, can I borrow your sable coat?"

"Oh sure. Just the thing for August."

"But I want to look glamorous—No! I won't betray the principles of Child Lib. I'll be *me.* But what is me?" She clasped her hands together and looked tragic. "There are so many me's struggling to express themselves. . . ."

Charlotte rolled her eyes.

"Is she to be believed? All right, Super-Brat. You've done enough acts for one day. Into bed. And turn off Star Trek."

"Not until Bill kisses me! I want all the world to know of our passion!"

I opened my arms. She ran into them, threw her arms around and hugged me. I felt her lips on my cheek. Suddenly she released me and moaned, leaning Garbo-like against the wall.

"It's too powerful for both of us," she sighed, and stalked tragically into her room, closing the door behind her. Just before it shut, she peeked out and winked at both of us. "If I become your mistress," she whispered, "I'd better warn you . . . I'm expensive."

"Nicky!"

"Good night," she cooed.

And the door shut.

Charlotte and I walked back to the stairs and descended them in silence. When we reached the circular foyer she took my hand. "Thanks," she said. There were tears in her eyes, which, thank God, she made no attempt to hide.

We stood there in the circular foyer, holding hands. We Americans, great inventors that we are, have never invented a successful compromise between the coldly impersonal handshake and the at times perhaps too personal mouth-kiss. It's probably some kind of hangup from our frontier mentality: either we want to keep a woman at a safe "proper" distance, or we want to "conquer" her. The hand-kiss is, of course, "furrin"; the Jet Set "social kiss" is somehow affected and unsatisfactory. I certainly wasn't thinking of "conquering" Charlotte at that point, but I felt so much for her I wanted to do something more than merely hold her hand. I took her in my arms and held her tight to me for a moment. It was the right thing to do. I could feel her relax. She *needed* someone to hold on to, someone to hold her

We stood that way a moment, then I released her. And then, without thinking, or rationalizing, I took her face between my hands and kissed her on the mouth. I think she wanted me to because at first she seemed to relax even more, but then she pushed me gently away and shook her head. "Not now," she whispered. "Please. Good night."

"Good night," I said, knowing of course that she was right. I gave her hand a final squeeze, and left the apartment.

Back at my hotel I had a world's championship rotten time getting to sleep. Charlotte and Nicky, Nicky and Charlotte. Everything else, including politics, suddenly seemed profoundly insignificant. When I finally got to sleep around three I had a terrible dream. I was in one of those TV-commercial meadows filled with wild flowers, and a girl was dancing toward me in TV-commercial slow motion. When she came close I saw it was Nicky. She smiled at me, then suddenly vanished.

I woke up in a sweat, and it took me at least another hour to get back to sleep.

It was one of the worst nights of my life.

Chapter
7

Tony Gleason lives in Brooklyn Heights, but by
eight o'clock he was at the Dorset suite. "Sit up
and open your baby blues," he said, shaking me.
"We've got to go over today's schedule."

"I know today's schedule," I groaned. If
there's anything I hate, it's being waked up by
schedules. "Tonight's the Norwegian-American
Banquet honoring the sesquicentennial of the
first Norwegian immigrants to the United
States. How can I honor a sesquicentennial when
I can hardly pronounce it?"

"All you have to say is, all you are you owe

to your Norwegian great-grandfather. Look ethnic, talk ethnic, eat herrings and get the Norwegian vote. Thank God you're blond." He straddled a chair as I put the pillow over my head.

"Go away," I said. "I'm tired. I need sleep."

"You can sleep in the Senate. You know about the show at ABC this afternoon. You have to be there at one-thirty. Now, this morning at nine we go to the East River heliport for an airborne inspection of Long Island Sound to check water pollution progress."

"Does water pollution progress mean more water pollution?"

"You know what it means. At noon we meet at Manny Hanny for lunch and a panel discussion of economic trends . . ."

"You'll have to cancel Manny Hanny."

"Huh?"

"I said, you'll have to cancel it. I can't make it."

Even under the pillow, I could feel the glare of his vote-tabulator eyes.

"And might I ask why?"

"I have another lunch date."

"Oh, you have another lunch date. Of course, I assume it's someone more important than the president of Manufacturers Hanover Bank and his panel of economists? Like maybe God?"

"It's an eleven-year-old girl named Nicky."

"You've got to be kidding."

I removed the pillow and sat up. "Look, Tony, I respect you as a campaign manager, I know everything you're about to yell at me is right, but there are certain things that are more important than lunches with economists, and I give you my word this is one of them."

"It's that goddamn Miss Face Cream, isn't it? You're banging her!"

"No, I'm *not* banging her."

"Then who the hell is Nicky?"

"Her daughter."

"Bill, are you going bananas on me? You couldn't have taken her to the goddamn zoo or something later this afternoon?"

"She wanted to go to lunch. I'm taking her. There's a good reason which is none of your business. And I *mean* it's none of your business."

He got up from the chair and went to the door. Then he looked at me. "First it was that dumb-ass Mercedes line—"

"Which didn't turn out so bad!"

"Maybe. We'll see. But now we've started canceling appointments. Okay, Bill, if you want to blow this campaign that's your business. But if you're not going to be a professional in this, then let me know now. Because I don't work for amateurs."

And he left the room, slamming the door behind him. I winced. I knew he was right. I was staking a lot on this campaign, and I knew that candidates simply don't cancel appointments.

But I also knew I wasn't going to disappoint Nicky.

To make things worse, I was late. As usual things had gotten fouled up, the helicopter almost crashed into Long Island Sound (thus producing an exotic new kind of pollution—politician-pollution), and when I stepped off the elevator into the black marble Egyptian foyer I was a bit off my feed. I rang the buzzer, thinking I had been stupid not to suggest a late-night movie after the Norwegian banquet instead. After all, Tony was right, the damn economists *were* important...

The door was opened by a pint-sized Sadie Thompson, or perhaps a miniature Bette Davis fresh out of "Of Human Bondage"—Nicky in a blond fright-wig with an Apache dancer black beret tilted over her forehead. Nicky in a black satin dress by Frederick of Hollywood. Nicky with ankle-strap Joan Crawford shoes, black net stockings, scarlet lipstick on her mouth and a black beauty spot on her left cheek. Nicky with her hands on her hips, her left hip jutting to the side like a Paris streetwalker out of some creaky thirties film.

"Allo, congressman," she purred. "You want make beeg love for leetle price, eh? Twenty francs for feefteen meenutes? I do massage, cheap." Wink.

"Yeah, okay. Beeg love leetle price, except

if you think I'm taking you to the Box Tree
dressed like that, you're crazy."

"You think I not good enough for fancy
restaurant, eh? You ashame of Fifi! go to 'ell!
Fifi got beeg class."

"Fifi got five minutes to change, or she can
eat at Nathan's Famous—solo. I've got to be at
ABC at one-thirty sharp."

"Merde! Fifi 'urr-ee! You wait! Fifi be right
back!" She ran to the stairs and started up,
stopping on the fifth step to wink down at me,
pull up her skirt slightly and show her leg.

"Sexy, eh? You die of desire, no?"

"I die of impatience. Come on, hurry up! I
passed up a bank president and six economists
for you."

"Fifi care *zat* for bank president!" she
sniffed, snapping her fingers contemptuously.
"And economists good for nozzing except beeg
recession." Then she raced up the rest of the
steps and vanished. I waited, wondering where
she had gotten that wonderfully sleazy dress.
In ten minutes she was running down the stairs,
wig gone, makeup off, now in a charming blue
dress and black patent leather shoes that made
her look very proper-little-Fifth-Avenue girlish.
The change was startling.

"How's this?" she asked, taking my arm.

"A little less flamboyant. Where did you get
that outfit?"

"Oh, there's a shop I know where you can
buy thirties- and forties-type stuff cheap. I went

out this morning and found it. Wasn't it perfect? Were you surprised?"

She was almost breathlessly eager for me to say yes. I hurried her to the elevator.

"Yes, I was surprised. You know something? You're more than a little bit nuts."

"I told you I was crazy, but isn't everyone? Don't tell me congressmen aren't crazy. Who gives the Pentagon all that money? You. I think you all ought to have your heads examined."

The elevator doors opened before I could think of a reply to that one—happily, because I happened to believe she was right. We rode down, Nicky chatting volubly with Charlie on the way, then got a cab and fifteen minutes later were being seated at the table I'd reserved at the tiny Box Tree restaurant by the headwaiter, with whom Nicky was babbling in French.

"Shall I order for both of us?" she said to me as the captain handed us the menus.

"Listen, Child Monster, when a gentleman asks a lady to lunch, the lady doesn't order unless she's Bella Abzug."

"I *like* Bella Abzug!" she snorted, suddenly looking very stiff and straight. "I suppose *you* hate her?"

I shook my head.

"No, I don't hate her. As a matter of fact, I admire her. The point I'm trying to make is, don't be so pushy."

I thought that since I was being a surrogate father, I was entitled to exert a little paternal discipline. She deflated. "I'm sorry. I *was* being pushy. From now on I'll be a perfect lai-dy. May I have a glass of wine?"

"No."

"Why not? Mother always lets me have one."

"You want this place to lose its liquor license?"

She gave in, without too much grace. I ordered a glass for myself, telling her I'd give her a sip on the sly, which cheered her. After the captain left us, Nicky looked around the room, which was filling up with the lunch crowd.

"I love this place," she said. "I think it's one of the prettiest restaurants in town, don't you? Do they have good restaurants in Washington?"

"Some, but it's not like New York."

She looked back at me.

"I've always thought it was so dumb to put the capital of the country *there*, don't you? I don't see why they didn't put it here, which would have made more sense. Why don't you introduce a bill saying the capital should be transferred to New York? That way the *Times* would be more friendly to the government and New York would have the whole federal budget to spend."

"And boy, would you spend it! Meanwhile, what would happen to Washington?"

"Turn it into a museum or something. Look! There's Jackie O! Oh, no it isn't. She just looks like her. I hate people that gawk at celebrities,

don't you? Tell me about your son," she rattled
on. "I'll bet he's a lot nicer than I am and probably a hundred times less radical."

"Are you radical?"

"Well, I'm a nihilist. How radical can you
get?"

"Are you a practicing nihilist?"

"I would be if I knew how. But I've never
figured out exactly what nihilists *do,* except
blow up tsars, which seems sort of pointless now.
What's your son's name?"

"Jeff."

"Is he sexy?"

I sighed. "Nicky, there are other things in
life—"

"What?"

I searched for an answer, but she beat me to
it. "Well, there's ballet. It's possible ballet's more
important than sex. Did Mother tell you she's
taking me to San Francisco the week after Labor
Day to see the Bolshoi Ballet? They're coming
from Russia on tour. Isn't that super?" She hesitated, then added, slyly, "Why don't you come
with us?"

"I can't. I have to be in Washington."

"But San Francisco's so romantic! Cable
cars and the whole schmeer . . ." She lowered her
voice to a whisper. "You and Mother could make
beeg love." She winked broadly.

"Look," I whispered back, "get that idea out
of your head, okay? Your mother and I are *not*
going to make 'beeg love'."

"Why not?"

"Because, among other reasons, I'm a politician and she's a very well-known lady, and if a politician and a well-known lady make 'beeg love,' people find out about it and it's 'beeg trouble.' "

"Thomas Jefferson had mistresses."

I sighed.

"Unfortunately, I'm not Thomas Jefferson."

She looked thoroughly disgusted with me.

"That's obvious," she sniffed, and picked up her menu. I did the same, then asked, "Figured out what you want?"

She put the menu back down and nodded. "The *quenelles de brochet* and the steak *au poivre*. That's one nice thing about being eleven, you can gorge and not worry about getting fat. But I'm really looking forward to fifteen. If you think I'm a Child Monster, wait'll you see me as a *teen-age* monster!" And she grinned evilly. The thought that she would never see fifteen flashed through my mind, and as quickly I instructed myself to forget it. So far, I thought I was doing pretty well. I wasn't going to spoil anything by even thinking the truth.

We ordered lunch after the wine. Then, at her prompting, I told her about Peggy and Jeff. She asked me so many questions about Peggy, I finally asked her why she was so interested in my wife.

"That's easy. She must be some fantastic

woman to keep you from falling in love with Mother."

"Fantastic? Well, she's—"

"She's what?"

"She's a good many things, including my wife," which I hoped would finish the subject.

She looked at me disdainfully.

"What a bore," she said, which, for her, did finish the subject.

She ordered an incredibly rich dessert— a *vacherin aux framboises* with *crême Chantilly* —and after she had galloped through it with gusto, she sighed contentedly.

"I adore good food," she said. "If I don't make it as a ballerina, I think I'll open a restaurant. A nihilist restaurant. Steak *bomb!*" She made an explosion sound that startled a gray-haired editor at the next table who was discussing an up-coming novel.

"Do you really want to be a ballerina?" I asked.

"More than anything else in the world. There's nothing more beautiful than ballet. I even think I may have been Pavlova in another life." She leaned across the table and dropped her voice to a throaty pitch. "Ven you look into my eyes, dollink, do you see the steppes of Rooshia?"

"Ven I look into my vatch, I see it's one-twenty and I've got to get to ABC, dollink."

She looked disappointed as I signaled for the check. I stared at it in horror; then, while I was paying, I noticed her watching the editor at the next table. She leaned over and said, "Excuse me, but this place is so small I couldn't help overhearing what you were talking about. You're in publishing, aren't you?"

The editor blinked with surprise as he looked at her.

"Well, yes . . ."

"Would you be interested in publishing my novel?" smiled Nicky sweetly.

"Your novel? You've written a novel?"

To my surprise, he looked interested. Then came the bomb.

"Yes, sir. It's a science-fiction novel, and it's called *Sex Slaves of Neptune*. It's about a planet that's ruled by fire-breathing lesbians, and they've enslaved all the men—"

"Nicky!" I was on my feet, hustling her away, smiling feebly at the dazed editor as I mumbled something about "brain fever." When I got her outside I said, "Now what the hell did you do *that* for?"

She was beaming.

"I wanted to see the look on his face. He about died!"

" '*Sex Slaves of Neptune*' . . . my God, where do you get stuff like that?"

"I didn't make it up. It's one of my father's novels. The title's better in French. If you can read French, I'll loan it to you. The covers are something else!"

"I'm afraid I don't know much about science fiction . . ."

"Oh, that's all right. Nobody knows his books." Then she added, rather defiantly, "He really was a super writer."

"I'm sure he was." I spotted a cab and quickly hailed it.

"Now, look, I'm going to be late so I'm putting you in a cab. Do you have enough money to get home?"

"Yes, but can't I come to ABC with you? Are you going to be on a show?"

"They're taping a talk show I'm on, and no, you can't come."

She looked disappointed. Then, as the cab pulled up, she smiled again. I lifted her up and she threw her arms around me and kissed me.

"It was a super lunch," she said. "Thanks. And aside from Mother, you're the best Adult Monster I know."

"And you're the best Child Monster I know."

"Really? Even better than Jeff?"

"He's not a Child Monster. He's just a kid."

"When will I see you again?"

I hesitated. "I don't know. I have to go to Washington tomorrow, and I'm not sure when I'll be back."

She frowned.

"But I *will* see you again, won't I?"

"Sure."

Suddenly, she looked very concerned. Again,

she hugged me tightly and whispered in my ear. "I love you. Please come back. Please."

I let her down. She looked at me a moment, almost accusingly, as if I were betraying her.

"I'll be back," I said. "Bet on it."

She looked relieved and, without another word, scrambled into the taxi. As the cab pulled away she raised both hands like claws, bared her teeth à la Dracula and made a monster face at me. I laughed and blew her a kiss.

Driving to the ABC studios, I thought of fire-breathing lesbians on Neptune and her beautiful eyes and the gusto with which she had eaten lunch and the delightful time I'd had with her, and I wanted to shake my fist at God.

Chapter
8

Nicky's repeated attempts to convince me to have an "affair" with her mother were forcing me to confront what my feelings really were toward Charlotte. I was attracted to her, I liked her, I was more than a little dazzled by her, and last but hardly least, I felt a great deal of compassion for her. I didn't think I was ready to jettison my whole past for her but I was definitely thinking about her more and more. And that night, at the Norwegian-American banquet, I had just enough vodka, wine and akvavit to propel me into a phone booth at the Waldorf and call her, even though it was close to midnight.

"It's your favorite congressman," I said when she came on. "Who's feeling all alone and lonely in the big city. Can I come over?"

"It's a little late, Bill . . ." I burped. "You also sound a bit bombed."

"You toast Norwegian-American friendship a dozen times with akvavit and you're not going to be sober. How about it? I'd like to see you. Very much."

"Give me fifteen minutes."

Twenty minutes later she was letting me in, and putting her finger to her lips.

"Nicky's asleep upstairs," she whispered. "Let's go out on the terrace."

I followed her through the half-dark apartment, past the enigmatic Kuan Yin and out to the terrace. It was a warm summer night. New York spread out below us, Central Park a black hole in the middle of a galaxy, with the distant Times Square an obscene supernova. The real stars above twinkled valiantly to compete, but they were no match for Con Edison. Still, the panorama was total magic, and Charlotte—splendid in a green silk pajama outfit, her blonde hair tied back with a green ribbon, her gray eyes watching me with half-amused curiosity—Charlotte was total withcraft. I took a deep breath to try to clear my head. Then I said, "I'm in love with your daughter."

She said nothing.

I put my hands on her arms and added, "The trouble is, I think I'm in love with you too." And I kissed her.

This time she didn't push me away, at least for a while.

Finally she whispered, "You're not really in love with me." She moved away to sit on the end of a wrought-iron chaise. "You've just been listening too much to Nicky. Or you feel sorry for her—and me."

"Of course I do."

"You've got a good marriage, you're on your way politically—don't mess it all up . . . Bill, I've already imposed on you enough and I don't want to drag you in deeper—"

"Maybe I *want* to be dragged in deeper. And don't tell me who I can or can't fall in love with—"

"Oh God, *don't*. Can't you see I'm messed up enough with Nicky?"

She stopped and put her hand over her eyes. I sat down beside her and took her in my arms. She put her head on my shoulder and I ran my hand down over her long, soft hair.

"I'm *trying* to keep you out of it," she whispered, "but you're not making it easy. Do you think Nicky's the only one who's flipped over you? Last Sunday when you made that crazy wonderful speech in Harlem—"

"Did you really like that speech?"

"Oh no"—she sighed—"he has to have his ego boosted when I'm trying to tell him I love him. Yes, I really liked that speech; it had balls. But I'm trying to tell you it's not right, it's not fair to you—"

"Let me worry about that."

Now, I suppose I should have made some effort to hold back. After all, I had been married eighteen years to Peggy, I had a close relationship with my son . . . these things should have been important to me, and of course they were. Except what I was *feeling* as most important was Charlotte. I was in love with her—and love, right or wrong, seems to diminish everything else in importance. I suppose love is the most demanding, in a way even the most selfish, of emotions. . . .

I took her face in my hands and kissed her. "I love you, Charlotte."

She sighed. "I give up. This is crazy, and we're both going to be sorry, but I give up."

She stood up and took hold of my hand. I got up and followed her into the darkened living room, through the long corridor to the circular foyer. There, she turned on the light and started up the stairs. Suddenly she stopped—as if having second thoughts? "Remember," she whispered to me, "Nicky's asleep. I *don't* want her to know."

"My God, *she's* the one who's been trying to get us into bed ever since—"

"Oh, she just thinks it's smart to talk that

way. I don't want my daughter to think her mother is bedding down with every congressman who happens to be passing through—"

The way she said it rather irritated me. "I'm not going to tell her, obviously, but—"

She put her finger to my lips. "I'm sorry, I didn't mean that the way it sounds, it's just that I'm nervous and upset and . . ." She was standing on the step above me. Now she leaned down and kissed me. "I guess I'm not making much sense, but you do understand?"

She looked at me a moment, as if studying me. Then she said softly, "I really *am* in love with you, Bill."

I followed her up the stairs, and we were almost to the top when Nicky suddenly appeared above us. Nicky in her pajamas and bathrobe, her feet in furry white slippers. She was holding Zoltan in her arms. As I froze, she ran down the stairs past us, saying casually, "Zoltan's hungry, I'm getting him some milk. Good night, everybody."

She hurried past me, humming to herself and tickling Zoltan's ear. Then she was at the bottom of the stairs, making for the kitchen.

I turned to look up at Charlotte, who at first seemed stunned by the encounter. Then she shrugged with resignation.

"Well," she said, "she certainly knows now."

"Not only knows," I said. "She's celebrating."

We exchanged looks, and were smiling as we continued on upstairs.

Soft . . . Her bedroom was all soft blues, with a large soft blue bed floating over the soft blue carpet. She was beautiful, all soft pink and gold . . . and afterward she put her lovely soft hand on my cheek and whispered, "My sweet William. How I do love you, my sweet William."

"Sweet William? Isn't that a weed?"

"No, lunkhead, it's a flower. I love flowers and I love you, so from now on you're my sweet William."

We lay in each other's arms for a while. Finally she said, "Nicky tells me you have to go to Washington and you don't know when you'll be back."

"I don't. When I'm not in Washington I've got speaking engagements around the state."

"Then I've got to think up something to make sure you come back . . . I've got it!" She disentangled herself from me and sat up, her voice rising with excitement. "I'll give a fund-raising party for you! Isn't the contribution limit a thousand dollars?"

"Yes."

"Then we'll ask a hundred people at a thousand dollars a head. That will be a hundred thousand for your campaign and my contribution will be the cost of the party. We'll have it here and I'll give you my A List, which is everyone worth knowing in this burg. It'll be a fabulous bash, and this way you'll have a perfectly legitimate excuse to come back. . . ."

I sat up. "Are you serious?"

"Naturally."

"But do you think there are a hundred people in New York who'd pay a thousand dollars to meet *me?*"

"Of course not. They'll come because I ask them. When you're elected, you'll be the main attraction. Until then . . . well, just you be here. And don't get drunk and drop your pants or something. Come to think of it, maybe you should drop your pants. Some of the people on my A List would be interested." She looked at me. "What's wrong?"

"Nothing's wrong."

"Oh, come on, Bill," She hesitated. "Of course, Peggy's invited too." She didn't sound overly enthusiastic.

"Well, she probably won't come, but it's not that . . ."

"Then what is it?"

I paused a moment, saying nothing.

"Shall we forget it?" she said. "I don't mean just the party."

I looked at her, silhouetted against the dim city-light coming through the curtained window beyond her. I reached my hand out and ran it slowly down her side.

"It's not just that I don't want to forget," I said. "I honestly don't think I could."

Chapter
9

But in the next two weeks I told myself I had to forget her. As much as I loved her and missed her; as much as I loved Nicky and missed *her;* still, the duplicity was eating at me. I guess it sounds almost absurd to say that a politician could worry so much about something so relatively minor on the current list of political sins as adultery. Today politicians are often held in such contempt—and for good reasons—that adultery almost seems wholesome. Almost. But it did worry me. As I said, I have to believe in myself, and now I was beginning to have doubts. If I could deceive Peggy, who else could I deceive?

So the choice came down to: either tell Peggy the truth and accept the consequences, or forget Charlotte. Night after sleepless night I worried the alternatives. I told myself again and again I had to make a decision. And yet when the first opportunity arose to do so, I didn't.

As I told Charlotte, I had several speaking engagements that brought me back to New York from Washington, and one was in West Schuyler itself. West Schuyler has a population of 6,354, and practically everyone in the town is a sports nut. Two years before, a drive had been started to raise a half-million dollars to build a swimming pool addition to the high school gym. I had been honorary chairman of the drive and arranged to get a third of the money from Albany, so when it came time to open the pool officially I was asked to be master of ceremonies. The event took place the following Saturday night, and West Schuyler put on a spectacular. Half the town was there, taking in the splendors of the eight-lane Olympic pool with its skylight overhead, and happily downing sliced ham, potato salad, baked beans and beer, courtesy of the local housewives and the fire department. The high school band marched around the pool play-

ing the national anthem, the "Stars and Stripes
Forever" and the high school song, "On, West
Schuyler, On, Pressing Ever Upward to Vic-tor-
ee," which had been written by the church or-
ganist in 1934 and was, by general consent, the
most unsingable high school song in the state
(the bass drummer narrowly avoided falling into the pool, which broke up the crowd). I made
a short speech praising everyone's efforts at
meeting the financial goal; and then, as flashbulbs popped, I cut the ribbon that had been
stretched across the shallow end of the pool,
following which we all retired to the bleachers
to watch the highlight of the evening—a display
of fancy diving and a swimming meet between
the West Schuyler team and a crackerjack outfit
from nearby Utica.

The meet was of more than routine interest
to Peggy and me because Jeff was on the relay
team. But as we squeezed between the mayor
and his wife to watch the fancy diving, my
thoughts were more on Nicky and Charlotte than
Eugenia Everts, West Schuyler's seventeen-year-
old diving whiz. As Eugenia did a spectacular
double-flip back jackknife, I thought of the
Nicky Dreyfus Fouetté Dive and reminded myself I had to decide between my old and familiar
and very comfortable world—a world I still respected and greatly valued—and a very different
life with Charlotte. I stole a look at Benita
Palmer, the plump wife of the mayor, who was
sitting next to me, and considered what *she*

would have thought of West Schuyler's representative in Washington if she'd seen him, only a week before, making love to a millionairess in a lavish Fifth Avenue triplex.

Just then Peggy turned and whispered to me, "A dime for your thoughts."

"A dime? What happened to the penny?"

"Inflation. You look about a thousand miles away."

"Oh it's just, uh . . . just some stupid campaign problem."

She squeezed my arm. "Well, forget the campaign. Tonight's your night to goof off. Oh look —there's Jeff."

Jeff was third man on the relay team. The race had started, and there was Jeff, his trim body poised on the starting box, ready to dive as the big electronic time clock flashed the miniseconds above the pool. As the number two man touched the edge of the pool, Jeff sliced into the water to start churning to the other end, his powerful arms and legs a marvelously efficient speed machine. The crowd went wild as he gained on his Utica counterpart. And when he overtook him, both Peggy and I were on our feet cheering and Benita was pounding my back and the mayor was hugging Peggy.

Jeff. How proud I was of him! Jeff, Peggy, the Palmers, West Schuyler . . . Once more I told myself I had to forget Charlotte.

Once more I couldn't quite bring myself to do it.

I had purposely avoided mentioning Charlotte's fund-raising party to Peggy, not only because I had been in Washington but also because frankly I was extremely nervous about Peggy's reaction. Now, as we drove home from the gym, I finally brought it up.

"Remember my mentioning that I'd met Charlotte Dreyfus?" I said.

"Yes."

"Well, she's giving a party for me the Tuesday after Labor Day. A fund-raiser at a thousand bucks a head."

"A *thousand?* You're kidding."

"Nope. She called me this morning in Washington and said they've already gotten over fifty acceptances."

"Where's it going to be?"

"In Charlotte's apartment, which is also quite a spread—"

"Oh? You've seen it?"

I tried not to react to the edge in her voice. "She asked me over last week to talk about plans for the party . . . she wants to know if you'll be there . . ."

"I wouldn't miss it for the world."

I shouldn't have been surprised, but I was. "You mean you *will* come?"

"Well, you always want me to help you campaign, don't you? And I certainly wouldn't miss meeting Charlotte Dreyfus. Of course I'll have to buy a new dress. I'm not going to have her think I'm some upstate frump." She paused, then added, "I want you to be proud of me."

That edge again? I wondered if Peggy—who's nobody's fool—had already guessed. Whether she had or not, here surely was the perfect opportunity to tell her.

Except I didn't.

What I said was, "I'm glad you'll be there."

There was silence for a moment, and then she laughed, quietly, almost privately.

"What's funny?"

"Oh, I don't know, all this talk about a party and a new dress made me think about that awful dress I wore at the senior prom—God, *that* sounds like something straight out of an old Snooky Lanson 'Your Hit Parade' number, doesn't it? Remember? It was the night Marty Palmer got bombed on rum and Coke and spilled his drink all down my front and—"

"And I got sore and slugged him?"

"Yes . . . oh, it was beautiful! And I was so mad at Marty! I thought that dress made me look like Grace Kelly—"

"You *did* look like Grace Kelly."

"Thanks, darling, but let's not get carried away." She paused, then: "And now Marty's the mayor and you're running for the Senate and Jeff's practically a grown man . . ." She shook her head. "Twenty years. It really doesn't seem possible."

I looked at her. In the dashboard glow, she looked eighteen again.

I think it was then I finally made my decision.

The Friday before Labor Day I took the shuttle from Washington to New York, but rather than flying straight on to West Schuyler I drove into Manhattan to Charlotte's office. Somehow, I had to tell her what I'd decided. It wasn't the easiest message to convey under the best of circumstances, and with Nicky's illness, this was hardly the best of circumstances for Charlotte. The elevator took me to the fortieth floor of the glass-box office building where the world headquarters of Marguerite Dreyfus Cosmetics were located. I stepped into the reception room and looked around. Suede walls, suede sofas, quasi-invisible pinpoint spots bathing everything in a murky penumbra of swank. Stainless steel doors behind a stainless steel desk where a gorgeous stainless steel receptionist looked at me beneath plucked eyebrows and ice-blue eyelids.

"Yes?" she drawled. Her Mandarin-length fingernails were lacquered pink.

"Congressman Dalton to see Miss Dreyfus."

"Do you have an appointment?"

"No."

"One minute, please."

Appraising me with all the warmth of a customs official, she dialed the inner sanctum while I looked at a big stainless steel and glass display case filled with samples of some of Charlotte's hundred-odd products. Ambience Perfume,

Star-Glow Eye Shadow, Milky Way Skin Moisturizer, Pulsar Lipstick, Galaxy Hair Lightener.
The brand names were all so intergalactic I wondered if Charlotte, like her daughter, was a fan
of her ex-husband's science-fiction novels. Finally a breathy voice behind me whispered, "This
way, congressman," and I turned to see an attractive Sarah Lawrence type in a jeans suit and
tinted pilot glasses smiling at me. I followed her
through the stainless steel doors (which slid silently shut behind us, like something out of
"Star Trek") down a long hall whose walls were
hung with framed blow-ups of Marguerite Dreyfus ads. A dozen doors along the way opened to
reception rooms of executive offices, but the big
bang was saved for the end of the corridor,
where yet two more stainless steel doors slid
noiselessly open and we entered Charlotte's outer office. Here a time-warp wrenched us back
to the twenties. Art Deco seemed to have taken
over with a vengeance. The walls were paneled
light with dark horizontal stripes; the ballooned
chairs were flame-stitched, and the tall, narrow
wall fixtures had twenties-style nymphs etched
into the smoked glass. It was effective, but I
didn't much like it. It struck me as style in search
of substance, which often is a New York City
disease. I suppose some would counter that West
Schuyler was substance in search of style and
not very actively searching at that. Once again
I was reminded of how different Charlotte's
world was from mine.

Finally I was ushered into the inner sanctum, where the twenties vanished to be replaced by Eighteenth-Century England with warm paneled walls. Hepplewhite sofas, oriental rugs and an Adam mantel over a fake fireplace. And then I saw Charlotte. In her pale pink dress with her blonde hair and her long elegant legs she could easily have been one of the models in her own ads. She came up to me and took my hands. "It's true," she whispered with a smile.

"What's true?"

"You're as gorgeous as I remember. I was afraid that Prince Charming in my bed last week might have turned into a frog."

"He has."

She let my hands go and I walked across the office to one of the floor-to-ceiling windows. I stared out at Park Avenue, forty floors below, feeling rotten. "How's Nicky?" I asked.

"It's hard to tell."

"What do you mean?"

"I'm afraid she's guessed the truth. I'm not sure but . . . well, I just sense it. She's putting up a front because she doesn't want . . . you know, pity. And I'm putting up a front . . . I don't know, maybe it would be better if I were open about it. Maybe I could help her. Except I'm not sure she wants help."

"Then maybe the best thing is to let *her* bring it up."

"Maybe you're right. At any rate I'm not going to do anything until after the party. She's so looking forward to it. . . ." She paused a moment, then added, "Aren't you going to kiss me?"

I didn't answer.

"What's wrong?"

Her voice was soft and, I thought, apprehensive.

"Peggy?"

Again I didn't answer.

"I knew this would happen."

I finally turned around. She was sitting on the sofa.

"It's not just Peggy," I said. "It's a lot of things. It's this funny image I have of myself as some sort of Mr. Clean to the voters. It's your money—"

"My money?" she interrupted. "What's that got to do with it?"

"A lot. I wanted to get you a present to thank you for giving the party but I couldn't think of anything to buy you. What do you buy the woman who's got everything?"

As always, mention of her money put her on the defensive.

"I don't want to talk about money—"

"But I have to be realistic!"

"I *hate* being realistic. I love you and that night you said you loved me . . ."

"I did, and I do. But I've got a wife and a son and a campaign. You've got Nicky—"

"What's Nicky got to do with it?"

"Maybe I'm looking good to you now because you've been so wiped out by what's happening to her." I slumped down on the edge of her desk, already having second thoughts. Finally I mumbled, "Shit."

"Mr. Clean shouldn't use four-letter words."

"Love's a four-letter word. God, I don't know where I am. When I'm home I think you and I are wrong. And when I'm with you—"

"Oh, Bill, don't. Don't make yourself miserable, which doesn't help either of us."

"But I'm right, aren't I?"

"I suppose. You're really a very decent man."

"Thanks for nothing."

"It's not nothing. Decency's become a rare commodity. It's also very frustrating."

We looked at each other.

"So we're decent," I said. "And we're nowhere. Wonderful."

She said nothing for a moment. Then, "Is Peggy coming to the party?"

"Yes."

"Do you think Jeff might want to come too?"

"I don't know. Why Jeff?"

"Nicky wants a date. She's got a huge crush on you, so she probably figures your son's the next best thing. Will you ask him?"

"Of course. He'd get a kick out of it."

We looked at each other across the office.

"I don't like being a frog," I said. "I'd rather be Prince Charming."

She shook her head as she stood up. "No, you were right. We'll blame it all on the akvavit."

End of the affair.

Chapter
10

I spent Labor Day weekend with Peggy and Jeff, and I explained to both of them about Nicky. Jeff in particular seemed upset by her sickness. Maybe it was because he was not that much older than Nicky; but I think it was more that Jeff, beneath his casual exterior, is a sensitive young man and the thought of anyone dying—much less an eleven-year-old girl—is abhorrent to him. I think that was why he was at first reluctant to be Nicky's date. As sympathetic as he was, instinctively he shrank from her and what she represented. It was an honest reaction. Most of us,

consciously or otherwise, mark those we know to
be seriously ill as "different." We know they are
slowly withdrawing from the world of the living
into the half-world of doctors and hospitals on
their way to that other world we all end up in.
Unfortunately, when they need us the most we,
with our own fears and insecurities, find it most
difficult to help—certainly Charlotte was going
through the same experience. In Jeff's defense
he must have realized this because later he came
back to me and said he'd be glad to go. He
wanted to "help." I thanked him but I also warned
him the last thing he was to do was let Nicky
think he was "helping." He understood.

The weather that weekend was beautiful,
and Peggy had asked a half dozen of our friends
over for dinner Saturday night. I'm a good bar-
becue chef, and as everyone gathered in the back-
yard I put on the steaks, mixed drinks and played
the genial host. But it was a forced act. Now that
I had broken off with Charlotte, I found I wanted
her that much more. Peggy, experienced at
reading my moods, at one point came over and
said, "Is something wrong?"

"No. Why?"

"You look sort of murky."

"I don't feel murky."

"Anyway, Sam wants his steak medium,
and Beverly wants hers burned to a crisp. It's a
sin to burn steaks, but what can you do with
Beverly? And you *do* look murky. Are you sure
I can't get you an aspirin or something?"

"No, thanks."

She gave me a curious look, then went into the kitchen to bring out the salad. It was hardly an earthshaking encounter, but it was the tremor before the quake.

The night of the party, by the time our car pulled up behind a gasaholic limousine, a crowd of onlookers and reporters had already gathered in front of Charlotte's building. We were late. I was supposed to be there at seven-thirty, but Jeff had lost one of his cuff-links at the hotel and it had taken us twenty minutes to find it (in his toothbrush case, of all places). So people were already arriving and flashbulbs were popping as we got out of the cab. The reporters didn't show any interest in us but they were having a field day with a couple that hurried into the building before us. I didn't know who they were, but they were obviously someone of importance; and when we rode up in the elevator with them I was amused to overhear the following exchange between them:

Mrs. Thin (in bored Park Avenue drawl): "Who *is* this Congressman Dalton?"

Mr. Thin: "Some hick from upstate."

Mrs. Thin: "Well, Charlotte better have some decent bubbly for a thousand dollars."

Mr. Thin (grimly): "It's tax deductible."

We were standing behind them, and I couldn't resist tapping Mr. Thin's shoulder. As he turned to look at me I smiled pleasantly and said, "I wouldn't vote for Dalton. I hear he's for confiscatory income taxes and redistribution of the wealth."

Mr. Thin blinked and turned slightly pale.

"They *all* are," he muttered sadly. "But thanks for the tip."

As Jeff choked back a laugh the elevator stopped and the door opened to a well-dressed mob that was pushing its way through the Egyptian foyer into the apartment. Charlotte had sent me a guest list for briefing purposes, so I had an idea of who had paid a thousand dollars to honor the "upstate hick" (the grand total collected was, incredibly, a little *over* a hundred thousand). It was a glittery mix of old money, new money, the press, show biz, Wall Street, "society" and the arts. It was a foreign world to me, but a world only an eremite or a Marxist would deny held a certain fascination. At risk of "upstate hick" brand of name-dropping, the list included Marie-Hélène de Rothschild, the de la Rentas, the Sulzbergers, the Houghtons, the Paleys, Estée Lauder, Kitty Carlisle, Lee Radziwell, Diana Vreeland, Andy Warhol, Barbara Walters, Lauren Bacall, Diane von Fürstenberg, Warren Beatty, the Buckleys, Joe Namath, Beverly Sills . . . that should give a flavor. At Washington parties you meet politicians and diplomats, lawyers and lobbyists—everyone in one way or another connected to Big Daddy in that one-industry town, and the mix tends to be flat because everyone does nothing but talk business: *the* business, politics. But New York has glamor, excitement and wit. I began to think Nicky was right—it should be the capital of the country. At the time, New York was being set up by the Administration as the symbol of All That Was Wrong With America. Yet as I looked at this elegant crowd, I thought that the Administration was being pious and smug. While I wouldn't champion the way New York was managed, the city at least generated ideas and things of value to the whole country: books, fashion, culture. What did Washington generate? A swelling bureaucracy, too often ineffective laws and always monstrous budget deficits. Compared to Washington's budget deficits, New York's relatively few billions looked like peanuts.

We finally reached Charlotte, who was kissing Mrs. Thin's cheek. When she spotted me, she said, "Where have you been? You're the guest of honor!"

Mr. and Mrs. Thin stared at me with amazement as I introduced Jeff and Peggy. Charlotte was breathtaking in a white evening dress that had some sort of silver thread woven into it so that she seemed to shimmer, and she was wearing what looked to be a fair share of the annual output of the Kimberley mines: a diamond and emerald necklace with matching earrings, two diamond bracelets and a diamond ring that would have inspired Raffles to concoct one of his more dazzling capers. That I had held this extraordinary person in my arms only a few weeks before and then let her go seemed almost incomprehensible.

She greeted Peggy and Jeff warmly, then instructed me to stand next to her to greet the incoming guests, who proceeded to look me over with polite curiosity. I knew they weren't necessarily endorsing my candidacy by paying a thousand each to eat mousse of smoked trout Anglais and saddle of lamb *aux fines herbes:* they were just covering all bets on the long shot that this upstate hick might end up in the Senate of the United States. As I pressed flesh and smiled, I reflected on how much I owed Charlotte for this party alone. Perhaps a cynic would say she was trying to "buy" me. But I remembered clearly that on the previous Friday when I went to her office and announced the "affair" was over, she never once mentioned cancelling this undoubtedly expensive bash, or even suggested I owed her anything at all.

Today "class" has come to mean almost anything. But for me Charlotte defined it.

Forty-five minutes later, the guests all arrived, Charlotte said to me, "Let's go up and get Nicky. And wait till you see her, your eyes will pop."

I followed her up the circular stairs to the second floor and we walked down to the door of Nicky's room. "Wait here," she said. "You're not allowed in the Child Ghetto until she gives you permission."

"Why?"

"When you see it you'll know."

She opened the door. Left alone in the hall, I looked toward the room opposite Nicky's. The door was open, and inside the dark room I saw what looked like a pale ghost. Rather startled, I crossed the hall and looked in, turning on the light. Then I realized the "ghost" was me; the wall was mirrored, and I'd seen my own reflection. In fact, all the walls were mirrored, and along one wall a long barre had been attached at waist height to the mirror. The only furnishing was a stool and a small table that held a phonograph. On top of it were LP albums: "Swan Lake," "The Firebird," "The Nutcracker," "Giselle" and something called "Practice Record." Above the phonograph was the sole decoration in the austere room: a taped-up poster of a ballerina, the photograph faded and obviously from another era.

"It's Pavlova."

I turned to see a Renoir child standing in the door. My eyes widened. I've said Nicky was a beautiful child, but in her simple, belted white dress she looked like an enchanted princess. She also had a look of slightly nervous expectation on her face that added an irresistible fawn-like quality. I wanted to freeze-frame her in my mind that way forever.

I whistled in admiration, and her face lighted up.

"Am I gorgeous?" she asked. "Is Jeff going to turn into a sex maniac when he sees me?"

"He's going to pant with passion and tear at you with his lust-crazed hands!"

"I can hardly wait!"

Charlotte appeared behind her.

"Okay, you, let's go downstairs. And *behave.* Jeff looks like a nice boy, and I don't want him to think I have Godzilla for a daughter."

Nicky blew a kiss at the poster.

"Wish me luck, Pavlova," she said. Then, as her mother took her hand, she assumed a tragic pose and sighed, "Tonight, I lose my virginity!"

"Nicky . . ."

"Let's go."

And she hurried into the hall. The three of us went down the stairs, Nicky between us, holding my hand. An orchestra was playing in the distance (I assumed it was on the terrace) and below us the Beautiful People were chattering, taking glasses of champagne from the trays the waiters were passing. Jeff was at the bottom of the stairs, talking to Peggy. When he saw Nicky, I could see he too was enchanted. When Nicky saw Jeff, it didn't take much guesswork to know what she was thinking. As usual, she blurted it right out.

"That's him, isn't it?" she whispered, squeezing my hand. "He looks just like you.

Sex City!" Then she spotted Peggy and mumbled, "And that must be the Enemy."

"The enemy?" I said, amazed. "That's crazy, Nicky. You'll like her."

"Oh yeah?" We had reached the bottom of the stairs. Now she let go my hand, flashed a phony smile and stuck out her hand to Peggy. "*Charmed* to meet you, Mrs. Dalton," she said, acting like Margaret Dumont in a Marx Brothers movie. "Your husband is *so* interesting, and I think it's fascinating that he's dedicated to the violent overthrow of the Government."

"Nicky, knock it off," snapped Charlotte. Then, to Peggy: "This, as you may have guessed, is sweet little Nicky."

"Hello, Nicky," smiled Peggy, shaking her hand. Nicky gave her a fishy stare.

"And this is Jeff," I said hurriedly.

She looked at all six feet two of him and sighed. "I think I'm going to faint. Are you a Marxist-Leninist or a Maoist-Socialist-Anarchist?"

Jeff looked helpless.

"I'm a Democrat," he confessed.

"Oh my God. Well, can you do the hustle?"

He cheered up. "Can you teach me?"

"I'd love to. Come on." She grabbed his hand and started pulling him toward the crowd, when suddenly she spotted someone and stopped, a look of shock on her face.

"It's *him*," she whispered. "It's actually

him! Oh, Mother, you didn't *tell* me! Joe Namath! Will you introduce me? Can I touch him?"

"*Maybe* I'll introduce you," said Charlotte, "if you behave."

"I'll behave! I'll take a blood oath! Do you think if I asked him he'd give me a lock of his chest hair?"

"Nicky," groaned Charlotte.

"But that's what everyone at school wants more than anything! And I'd frame it and wear it over my heart for*ever*. Come on, Jeff, let's go stare at him. If I fainted in front of him, he'd have to notice me, wouldn't he?"

And off they went. Peggy laughed rather dubiously. "Well, she's certainly . . . precocious, isn't she?"

"That's one word for it," said Charlotte dryly.

"I know Bill has already thanked you for the party," Peggy went on. "But I just wanted to add my thanks. It's a wonderful boost for his campaign, and the money—well, I guess I don't have to tell you how much that's going to help."

Charlotte looked at me and said very quietly, "Your husband is a fine man. He'll be an asset to the Senate."

It was so simply put and, I think, so genuine. Those warning lights were flashing in my brain again.

Whatever Charlotte or Peggy may have thought of each other privately, publicly they behaved with great charm. Charlotte took Peggy

and myself around the apartment, introducing
us to everyone, chatting with Peggy. Watching
them, you might have thought them old friends.

What worried me was what Nicky thought
of Peggy, whom she had declared the "Enemy."
With Nicky's repeated and unsubtle hints about
how she wanted me and her mother to be an
"item," it didn't take much imagination to figure
why Peggy was, in her eyes, the villain of the
piece. But since Charlotte and I *had* been an item,
and Nicky knew it, I began to wonder what Super-
Brat might be up to. It was she who had maneuvered my son to the party. Was it possible she
might tell him what had gone on that night, just
to cause trouble? I didn't *think* she would do it,
but . . . I decided to have a talk with the Child
Monster, and at the first opportunity I pulled
her away from Jeff and took her out on the terrace. She was drinking a glass of champagne.

"He's super!" she enthused, snatching two
hot canapes from a passing tray and popping
them into her mouth. "He's really cute and
smart and nice and has a *great* body. I think I'm
falling in love."

"Good. . . . Listen, Nicky, we're friends,
aren't we?"

"More than 'friends.' 'Friends' is a yucky
word. Actually, we're non-sexual lovers."

"Right. And people like us don't hurt each
other, do they?"

She looked at me coolly.

"Oh, I get it," she said. "You're afraid I'll tell

your wife about *that* night. What do you think I am, a fink? Besides, there isn't anything going on between you and mother anymore." She took another sip of champagne, then added, "Unfortunately."

I lowered my voice. "Nicky, what *is* it you want?"

And suddenly she became quite serious.

"You for a father," she said. "And a dynamite husband for my mother. And I'm going to get it, too."

She looked at me for a moment, very intently, then smiled and went back inside, leaving me dazed, touched, and rather depressed. For the fact was that at that point, I wanted precisely the same thing she did.

It came as no surprise that the head of a world-wide cosmetics empire should be an efficient party-giver: the party was run with the precision of one of Napoleon's campaigns. Fourteen round tables each seating eight were set up; eight on the terrace, four in the dining room and two in the library, place cards for everybody. Gorgeous flowers were everywhere, and hurricane lamps had been placed around the terrace floor (luckily it was a beautiful evening). The bandstand was on the terrace, in the middle of the Fifth Avenue side, and a bar was on the north side. With the city glittering like Tiffany's below, it was certainly a night to remember.

Promptly at nine, Charlotte passed the word that dinner was starting and led me to one of the terrace tables where she'd seated me between the queen of Paris society, the Baronne de Rothschild, and one of the queens of New York society, Babe Paley. She had also seated the publisher of the *Times* and his wife at the table, and I realized again that Charlotte was no amateur at the power game: an opportunity to express my views to the Sulzbergers couldn't exactly hurt. Unfortunately I didn't get much opportunity since Marie-Hélène de Rothschild, who'd grown up in New York, monopolized the conversation, going on about how she loved the city and how she and her husband Guy had just given Ferrières, the monumental 9,000-acre Rothschild estate outside Paris, to the French Government, not to mention the problems involved in moving into their new Paris townhouse, the historic Hôtel Lambert on the Ile St. Louis . . . well, it was all pretty heady, and it was comforting to know the Rothschilds had problems too. We were half-way through the mock turtle soup when Charlotte launched a surprise: models began appearing, stalking their way through the rooms and around the tables in that half-ridiculous, half-curiously fascinating high-fashion-model way of walking that I guess is supposed to convey elegant sexuality. The guests loved the unexpected show, and the models (there were ten, Charlotte later told me, and they used the bedrooms on the third floor for dressing

rooms) were gauntly beautiful. It was a great
show and I'd be a liar if I didn't admit I enjoyed
watching it as much as I enjoyed the beauty of
the setting, the food and the Lafitte-Rothschild
the waiters kept pouring in a red river. But I was
also thinking about that other New York, that
New York I'd taken my campaign to a few weeks
before. The New York of open hydrants and Reggae blaring from cheap radios on window sills.
The heckling woman, the leering wino, the smirking pimp in the Borsalino hat. If I were elected to
the Senate I wanted to represent those people as
well as the Paleys and Sulzbergers. Yet how
could anyone honestly represent the interests of
both, the bottom and the top of our social scale,
separated as they are by the entire structure of
our society and yet so dramatically juxtaposed in
this most crowded, most highly charged and undoubtedly most fascinating city in the country?
A good question, you may well say, and I didn't
have any good answer. But Charlotte had told me
the guests would expect a few pearls of wisdom
from me for their money, and I decided my theme
would have to be the same one I had used in
Harlem.

After the dessert I made a quick trip to the
john, then hurried back out to the terrace, where
Charlotte led me to the bandstand. Her introduction was short and sweet, and the guests crowded
the terrace to watch as well as listen.

"I don't have to tell you *my* choice for the
next Senator from New York," she said, speak-

ing into the microphone so that her voice reached those who had remained inside at their tables, "since I've already extracted a thousand dollars from each of you for his campaign. But I'm not going to try to sell you. I'll let him sell himself. Congressman Bill Dalton."

Polite applause as I took the mike from Charlotte, who sat down behind me on the clarinetist's chair.

"I want to thank our lovely hostess," I began. "And I want to thank all of you, not only for your contributions but for your interest. And this year, getting anyone interested in politicians isn't easy. The only interest I've noticed is a general desire to lynch *all* of us."

A few half-hearted chuckles, but I was becoming aware that something was wrong. If nothing else, politics teaches you to sense the mood of a crowd, and the mood of this crowd was mysteriously derisive. I noticed people smirking, whispering to each other. They knew something I didn't. I began to sweat.

"There are good reasons for this lack of interest," I went on, "and it's not just Watergate. Candidates for public office are fudging on the issues. The voters have split into so many fragmented groups that candidates are afraid to alienate that they end up saying nothing. The result isn't public debate. The result is baby food. Well, I don't think the people of New York are babies..."

I noticed Nicky signaling to me and lost my

train of thought. She was standing next to Jeff by the satyr's head basin and was mouthing something and waving her hand. I throttled my anger at her and tried to recover my fumbled sentence.

"Uh . . . I think the people of New York want issues, and . . . uh . . . certainly one of the main issues today is welfare. A few weeks ago I took my campaign to Harlem, where I made a speech. One result of that was a phrase, or slogan, that Mr. Sulzberger's paper labeled 'irresponsible.' The slogan was 'A Mercedes in every pot,' and it's true—it was irresponsible and misleading. But the idea, I think, is valid . . ."

I stopped. The tittering was spreading, and Nicky was driving me nuts with her signals.

"There seems to be a young heckler in the crowd," I snapped, glaring at her. "Nicky, *what* is wrong?"

She pushed through the guests to the bandstand, stood on her tiptoes, cupped her hands around her mouth and whispered in my ear, "Your fly's open."

A public speaker's nightmare come true. I turned around, my face crimson, and fumbled at my fly. It was wide open, though, thank God, nothing was showing. During my quick trip to the john I must have pulled the zipper off its track and hadn't realized it. As I fumbled at the damned thing I heard the snickers mounting. Finally, safely zipped, I turned back to face the people, who were now straining not to roar with laughter.

Shrugging helplessly I said, "Well, at least I'll get the flasher vote."

The house came tumbling down. People were doubling over with hilarity. I stood there, laughing myself, waiting for it to die down. When it did I found I had them on my side. I guess there's nothing to make people like you more quickly than a recovered fumble. They listened to the rest of my speech with respectful attention, and at the end gave me a warm hand. The subject wasn't much of a crowd-pleaser to begin with, so it turned out that the open fly was a blessing in disguise.

I decided I owed Super-Brat a kiss for her rescue.

But Peggy thought otherwise.

After my speech the orchestra began playing, the bar was reopened and politics were forgotten as people began dancing on the terrace. I returned to my table (where the Sulzbergers congratulated me on my speech) and found Peggy sitting alone, sipping coffee.

"How about a dance?" I said.

"No thanks."

She seemed cool, which is unusual for her. Sensing trouble, I sat next to her.

"I guess we'll have to invest in a new zipper." I grinned.

She didn't.

"Nicky didn't have to make such a big deal out of it. Drawing everyone's attention . . ."

"Oh, come on, everyone already knew. Everyone except me. Nicky saved the day."

"She's a show-off."

"No kidding. She's also spoiled, I guess, and I'm nuts about her."

"And she's nuts about you. That's obvious. It's also obvious she hates me, which is curious."

"She doesn't hate you . . ."

"She certainly doesn't like me."

She looked at me. Feeling a pit ominously opening at my feet, I decided to change the subject.

"Come on, Peggy, let's dance."

"Why don't you dance with the hostess?"

"Because I want to dance with my wife."

"Oh? Why?"

I leaned forward and lowered my voice. "Peggy, what's wrong?"

Her expression was a mixture of anger and hurt. "Don't you think I see what's going on here? I'd have to be blind not to, with the daughter so hostile and the mother being so charming—as she spends thousands on my husband."

All right. She knew. I wasn't going to insult her further by pretending ignorance or making some stupid denial.

"It *was* going on," I said. "I'll admit that. It's not anymore."

"Do you really expect me to believe that?"

"Yes, because it's the truth."

"Even if it is the truth, what's the difference? All it takes is once to break a trust." She shrugged. "Eighteen years. I suppose it's a miracle it lasted that long—"

"Peggy, this isn't the place—"

"Why not? In a way I suppose I don't blame you. She's beautiful, she's rich, she can do things for you I can't . . . oh, go ahead—*dance* with her, for God's sake. Make love to her. It's not the end of the world. I'll survive the glamorous Miss Dreyfus." She paused, then added, "But if you think I'm going to give you up without a fight, you're wrong, Bill. I've got eighteen years invested in you . . ."

I didn't know what to say, so for once I said nothing. I got to my feet. She watched me walk away from the table. This time, my fly wasn't open. This time, I was naked.

The orchestra was playing Cole Porter, and with the couples dancing on the penthouse terrace the setting was pure thirties. I suppose my dilemma was, too, but it was being played in the seventies: The wife—hurt, angry, betrayed. The husband—guilty, confused. And Charlotte? What was she thinking? She was behaving so well. Had she really closed the books on me, deciding that I'd been right and our relationship was a dead end? Or did she still want me as much as I wanted her? I didn't know. I didn't know what the hell to do.

I spotted Jeff. We had always been honest with each other, and I wanted him to know what was happening. He was at the side of the south terrace, talking to one of the models. I hated to cramp his style but I came over, said, "Excuse me," and took him aside.

"Can I talk to you for a minute?"

"Sure. What's up?"

I looked around. It was too personal to be discussed in the middle of a crowd, but at the east end, to the rear of the penthouse, the terrace was dark and empty. I led him back. He leaned against the brick parapet and looked out over the city.

"Some pad," he said. "And some party. I'm glad I got invited."

"What do you think of Nicky?"

"She's a sketch. I really like her."

"How about her mother?"

He looked at me.

"I like her too. What's with the Twenty Questions?"

I leaned against the wall next to him. In the distance, between the tall buildings, I could catch glimpses of the East River.

"Jeff," I said, "you know, you're pretty terrific, for a son."

"Sure, I know." He grinned.

"Well, I'm not so hot, as a father."

Cole Porter in the distance. Here, silence.

"Dad, if you're trying to tell me there's

something going on between you and Nicky's
mother, don't sweat it. I already know."

"How?" I was genuinely surprised.

"Nicky told me a while ago. Now, don't get
the wrong idea. She didn't actually come out and
say it, but we had a long talk and she admitted
the reason she really wanted me here tonight
wasn't just to meet me but to . . . well, sort of
alert me about what she's up to. I mean, that
she's trying to get you to marry her mother—"

"Then she *did* come out and say it?"

"Well . . . in a way. But I admire what she
was trying to do. She told me she didn't want to
. . . you know, mess up our family, and that if
I thought she was doing the wrong thing to tell
her and she'd stop. You know, for a kid her age
I thought it was pretty mature."

"What did you tell her?"

"I said I couldn't take sides. That I loved
you and Mother but that if you two weren't happy together anymore . . . well, I wasn't happy
about it but it was really none of my business.
And I believe that. I'm seventeen. I've got my
own life to lead. It's wrong for me to try to lead
yours."

"I'd still like to know what you think."

"You're putting me on the spot."

"You're right, I'm sorry."

He thought a moment.

"All right, congressman, Ill take a position.
Who are you in love with? Who do you really

want to be with? That's what's important, isn't it?"

"Maybe it is at twenty. When you're forty, I'm not so sure . . . but I guess that's my problem."

He put his hand on my shoulder. "You'll work it out, Dad."

He was putting me on, of course, and I suppose the reversal of the father-son relationship had its amusing aspects.

"I guess I haven't been too much help," he added. "Uh . . . if you don't need me . . ."

"Sure. Get back to your model. And thanks, Jeff."

Released from duty, he wasted no time returning to the action. I stood alone in the dark, watching the East River and listening to Cole Porter.

Ten minutes later I cut in on William Buckley, who was dancing with Charlotte. The columnist smiled superciliously at me and said, "Interesting idea, your family assistance plan. But Nixon thought of it first."

"I know. Too bad he was too busy picking locks to make it work."

Charlotte chuckled as we danced away to "From This Moment On."

"Well," she said, "you're a hit. Everyone's impressed. You got more mileage out of an open fly than Casanova. Congratulations."

"Thanks."

"Is Peggy having a good time?"

"A ball," I lied.

"She's really terribly nice. I like her . . . Will you be going back to West Schuyler tomorrow?"

"Yes. Then Washington."

"So we won't see you for a while?"

I realized, with sudden panic, that it was all over and this was her way of saying good-by. Except the last thing I wanted was to say good-by.

"Nicky says you're taking her to San Francisco next week," I said casually.

"Yes, for three days. I have to go on business, and the Bolshoi's playing there. I thought she'd get a kick out of it. Besides . . . I want her to be with me."

"When are you leaving?"

"A week from tomorrow. Why?"

"I have to be in San Francisco a week from tomorrow. I'm on the Banking and Currency Subcommittee, and I'm meeting with a delegation of California bankers. What hotel are you staying at?"

"The Stanford Court."

"I'm staying at the Stanford Court."

"Maybe we'll bump into each other."

"Maybe."

"Is there a delegation of California bankers?"

"There is now."

"And why are you changing your mind?"

"Because I'm crazy about you."

The music segued to "It's Delightful, It's Delicious, It's De-Lovely."

I'd dreamed up the delegation of California bankers as a smokescreen for Tony Gleason, who I knew would raise hell if he found out I was going to California for any purpose not directly convertible into votes. I had no intention, though, of lying to Peggy. Now that everything was out in the open with her I was at least going to keep it that way. But when I went to look for her, Clyde told me she had gone back to the hotel. Well, I suppose I couldn't blame her. I was debating whether to return to the hotel myself when Nicky hurried up to me.

"You owe me a dance," she said, grabbing my hand. "Mother's making me go to bed, which is cruel and anti-Child Lib, and you haven't danced with me once."

"You're right, I'm a boor. May I have this dance?"

"Oh God, don't waste time! The Mother Monster's watching!"

She led me back to the terrace, where they were playing "Falling in Love with Love." "Do you waltz?" I asked, thinking I must sound to her like Prince Metternich.

"Of course I waltz. I do everything. I'm going to be a ballerina, remember?"

We began waltzing. Rather to my embarrassment, the other dancers stopped and formed a ring to watch the Congressman and Thumbelina do their thing. She was ecstatic.

"Look, they're all watching! Isn't that super? Do you think I should let Jeff kiss me?"

"Has he tried?"

"No, but he might. Oh, I'm only fooling myself," she added, glumly. "Jeff's been wonderful but he couldn't possibly be interested in me romantically."

"Jeff told me about your little chat." She looked apprehensive. "It was decent of you to warn the enemy you're about to declare war."

"Jeff's not the enemy."

"Nobody is."

"I know—I was rude to your wife. I'm sorry. I really am." Then she added, "Do you want me to apologize to her?"

"She's gone back to the hotel."

She guessed what had happened. "Oh God, I really got you in trouble, didn't I?"

"I already was. And my going to San Francisco isn't going to help."

Her eyes widened. "San Francisco? You mean you're going too?"

"I'll be there."

She looked ready to explode with excitement.

"Oh, talk about *su*-per! Talk about fan-*tas*-tic!"

"Okay, okay, knock it off." I saw Charlotte pointing at her daughter, mouthing "bed." "The Mother Monster just sent the signal."

"Oh no. Oh please, just one more dance?"

"No."

"Will you take me upstairs? Please? I'll show you my room."

"I was told only special people were allowed in the Child Ghetto . . ."

"If *you're* not special, who is?"

"Okay, it's a date."

The music stopped, as did we. The spectators broke into applause. Her face lighted up as she looked around the terrace at her audience. Then, delighted, she applauded back at them.

"They *loved* us! I'm a star!"

"You're also a ham. Come on. Bed time."

"Oh God, you're sounding just like a *parent*. I want a father, not a parent."

I led her over to Charlotte, who said, "Well, did you have a good time?"

"It was fabulous," said Nicky, kissing her. "You get A plus."

"Thanks, so do you. Where's Jeff?"

"Over talking with—sigh!—Joe Namath. Mother, would you let me try falsies?"

"*No.* Now, come on, let's go up—"

"You stay here. Bill's going to take me."

"All right, but only five minutes. Don't try to use him to stay up."

"Oh, Mother, that would be dishonest, and you know I'm *never* dishonest."

"You lie like a rug and you know it. Good night, darling. You were beautiful tonight."

The compliment pleased Nicky, who blushed,

suddenly acting her age. Then, eyeing me with a triumphant gleam, she whispered something to Charlotte, who smiled. She started humming "California, Here I Come" as she hurried over to Joe Namath, who was talking to Jeff.

"Mr. Namath," she said, "can I have a lock of your hair? Just a little lock? You've got so much hair you couldn't possibly miss *one* lock?"

Namath grinned and yanked a hair from his head.

"Why not?" he said. Nicky took it, holding it with such reverence it might have been a piece of the True Cross. I was glad she had settled for a scalp hair instead of the chest variety.

"Thank you," she breathed. She tucked it in a pocket of her dress. Then she kissed Jeff. "I've got to go to bed now," she said. "But thanks for being my date." Then she was off again, still humming, "California, Here I Come." I followed her through the crowd to the foyer and we hurried up the stairs. Reaching the second floor, she sprinted down the long hall, stopping in front of the mirrored room, which she entered. When I reached the door I looked in to see her collapsed on the floor. At least, at first I thought she was collapsed. Then I realized she was posing, her legs in a split, her face down and almost pressing against her right knee, her two arms stretched over her head across her outstretched leg, her clasped hands on the floor. Then, slowly, she raised her arms and body, moving with exquisite

grace. When she was upright, she smiled at me.
"The Dying Swan," she said. "Pavlova danced
it at the Maryinsky Theatre. And *we're* going
to see the Bolshoi in San Francisco!"

She scrambled to her feet. "This is my
practice room. Mother put it in for me. You
know, she's terribly generous and she's got *tons*
of money. You're nuts not to marry her."

"Look, Nicky, don't push your luck."

She laughed and came over to take my hand.

"All right. But I'm doing pretty good so far,
aren't I? Come on, I'll show you the Child Ghetto." She led me across the hall. "Now you've got
to realize this isn't the *real* me anymore. I'm
much more sophisticated now. What you're going to see is the *old* me, which was childish."
Giving me a sultry look as she opened the door, she
added in her mock-Garbo bit, *"Now* I am a vo-man."

She went into the room, took a look around,
sighed and looked helplessly back at me.

"Oh, it's so beautiful. No, it *is* the real me."

I went into the room and gaped. Obviously
Charlotte had at one time tried to give her
daughter a pretty-little-girl room. Here and
there I spotted patches of flowered wallpaper,
and white curtains swooped across the windows.
But it had been a lost cause: the Child Monster
had struck. Old movie posters were everywhere,
with horror and science fiction predominating.
"Dracula," "Frankenstein," "The Mummy,"
"The Mummy's Tomb," "The Mummy's Hand,"
"Day of the Triffids," "Forbidden Planet,"

"White Zombie," "2001," "The Day the Earth Stood Still," "Godzilla," "It Came from Outer Space," "The Thing" . . . all mixed in with "Casablanca," "The Maltese Falcon," "Dr. Strangelove" and other pop favorites. Pinned to the curtains were two huge "Star Trek" posters of Captain Kirk and Mr. Spock. By her fourposter bed stood a lobby display cut-out of King Kong, while next to her desk another life-size cut-out of a red-caped Bela Lugosi bared his Dracula fangs, thirsting for a high-calorie blood lunch. On her desk, which was piled with comic books and junk, a plastic statue of the Mummy lurched menacingly next to the mother lode of all this pop horror detritus, a Sony TV set. The only what might be called "little girl" touch in the whole bizarre room was a cardboard box on the floor, under the picture of Captain Kirk in which four kittens were crawling about.

I burst into laughter. "Who's your decorator —Boris Karloff?"

She went to the kitten box.

"Me—I'm the decorator. Isn't it fantastic?" She scooped one of the kittens from the box and cuddled it. "Oh, Micuse, *tu petit méchant, je t'aime. As-tu faim, méchant?*" Then she looked at me. "My favorite's the Mummy. Isn't he cute? When he gets homesick I take him down to the Egyptian foyer and boil him tana leaves."

"What are tana leaves?"

"They bring mummies back to life. He's searching for his long-lost love, the Princess

Anakhon. You see, this dumb archeologist broke the sacred seals of his tomb and that caused the curse to start, so he has mixed feelings about archeologists. But he's nice to other people. *Bonne nuit*, Micuse." She gave the kitten another kiss and replaced her in the box. Then she came over and stood in front of me, looking at me rather strangely. I squatted down to be at her height, and I took her hands.

"Do you really like my room?" she asked.

"I love it. It's like you—crazy."

Suddenly she put her arms around me and hugged me tightly. I hugged her back. Then she said, softly, "Will they let me stay here at the end, or will they make me go to the hospital?"

It came as a complete shock, and hit me like a fist in the stomach. My mind raced to try and find the right thing to say, for I knew she was committing the ultimate act of trust.

"Do you want to talk about it?" I asked.

"I don't know." She paused. "Yes, a little. With you. I don't want to talk about it with Mother. She'd get too upset."

"Your mother's a tough lady ..."

"No she isn't. You don't know her like I do. I saw her go to pieces when she broke up with my father, and then when that second creep she married left her . . ." She released me and looked at me. Her face, usually so animated, had become very serious. "Don't you see," she said, "that's why it's so important for me to get *you* for her. Because I know that ... later on Mother's

going to really crack up unless she has someone to hang on to. She'll need you." She hesitated, and for a moment I thought she was going to cry. But she fought it back. "And *I* need
you now," she added softly. "I'm trying to be
. . ." she shrugged ". . . you know, 'brave' and
all that, but it's not so easy. If you want to
know the truth, I'm scared."

I was trying not to cry, but I wasn't doing
a very good job of it. I felt so much love for her.
The tears started down my cheeks. I took her
in my arms again and hugged her, partially so
she wouldn't see the tears and mostly because
I wanted to.

"It's the hospital—*that's* what scares me,"
she whispered. "Will you come with me if I have
to go?"

"Yes, I'll come with you."

"Is that a promise?"

"That is a promise."

I released her, and she looked at me for a
moment. Then she said, "You know, God's given
me a shitty deal. But he's given me you at the
end, and that makes up for something."

And then, as if wanting to break off the sub-
ject, she looked at the clock next to the Sony.
"It's eleven-thirty. I'm going to watch 'House of
Frankenstein.' You won't tell Mother, will you?"

"You can trust me." I squeezed her hand.
"Good night, Super-Brat. I love you."

I went to the door and opened it. Before I
left, I looked back. She was standing in the middle

of the room, watching me. She looked very alone.

"See you in San Francisco," she whispered.

I blew her a kiss and went out in the hall, closing the door behind me.

I felt numb.

It was almost midnight. As I went downstairs I heard the orchestra still playing but the guests were starting to leave. I spotted Charlotte at the bottom of the stairs talking to Diana Vreeland. When she saw me, she came over and said, "Is she in bed?"

"Yes," I lied.

"She's not going to watch television?"

"No."

"You're lying."

I shrugged. "Caught. She wants to watch 'House of Frankenstein.' Why don't you let her? It couldn't hurt."

Charlotte shook her head. "She's got you hooked."

"I know. Listen, Jeff and I have to get back to the hotel. You knew that Peggy already left?"

"No. I didn't see her . . ."

"She's not too happy. She knows."

"Oh." She hesitated. "Well, I'm sorry. But I'm not sorry you're coming to San Francisco. That's the nicest present you could have given me."

I looked around. Mrs. Vreeland was talking to someone else, but she was keeping her eye on Charlotte and me. Then I spotted the small elevator under the circular stair.

"Does that elevator of yours work?" I asked.

"Of course."

"Why don't you take it to the second floor? There's a surprise for you up there."

She understood. She got into the elevator, closed the cage and pushed the lever. It slowly ascended. I went to find Jeff and told him to meet me in front of the building in ten minutes, then hurried to the kitchen and took the servants' stairs to the second floor. I ran down the corridor to the elevator. Charlotte was inside, waiting. I squeezed in beside her and pushed the lever. The door shut and we started to the third floor. Halfway up, I pushed the "stop" button and the tiny cage bumped to a halt. I put my arms around her.

"*Got* you."

"You're totally insane," she said as I began kissing her.

"Well, you said private elevators are decadent," I mumbled.

Five minutes later I brought the cage back down to the second floor and got out.

"San Francisco," I said in a low voice. "The Stanford Court. A week from tomorrow."

"You've got lipstick on your mouth," she whispered back. I took care of it with a handkerchief and looked at the red.

"Revlon?"

"Drop dead."

The elevator door closed, and she blew me a kiss as she slowly sank out of sight.

Someone once wrote that the test of a good marriage is whether the husband and wife sleep together in the nude. Well, for eighteen years Peggy and I had slept in the nude. But when I got into our bed at the hotel a half hour later, I wished for pajamas.

Peggy was on her side, her back to me, pretending to be asleep. I knew that she wasn't. I put my head on my pillow and stared at the dark ceiling. Finally I said, "Don't you think it was a bit abrupt taking off like that?"

"What was I supposed to do, thank the hostess for stealing my husband?"

"She hasn't exactly stolen me."

"Oh? I'm delighted to hear it. What happens now?"

"I'm meeting her next week in San Francisco."

Silence.

"I don't know whether . . ."

She finished the sentence for me. "Whether you're going to marry her?"

"Yes."

"But you're thinking about it?"

"Yes."

"So this is more than a turning-forty fling."

More silence. Then, finally, she said, "Thanks at least for being honest."

And nothing more was said. What more was there to say?

Chapter
11

The amount of drunkenness in Washington is, quite literally, staggering: the number of top-level politicians and bureaucrats who are heavy drinkers would surprise even the most hardened cynic. Whether it's the pressures of the game or of political ego that cause the boozing, I'm not sure—maybe it's both. But Washington boozes. And, since Watergate, as Washington has become increasingly aimless and alienated from the country it's supposed to represent and govern, Washington has boozed more and more. Obviously I can't—and won't—name names, but one man comes to mind who has graced a number of the highest jobs in Washington and whose public image is one of intelligence, integrity and class (pretty rare in a politician). Yet he is so hooked on wine (fine wines, give him that . . . he really knows the poison that's killing him) that he has refused a better-than-average shot at the White House because he couldn't take the thought of having to stay sober through all those long state banquets.

I mention this because the following week, which I spent in Washington, I became aware that whispers were starting about me. Whispers not about my drinking, but about the fabulous party given for me by Charlotte Dreyfus and the amount of money raised for my campaign by her and just why was a glamorous cosmetics tycoon suddenly knocking herself out for Bill Dalton? People involved in the power game have a passion for gossip, and here was a true feast for the gossip mongers. The talk increased when the party was written up in *Newsweek*. The biggest names on the guest list were mentioned, and of course the presence of celebrities and showbiz types at a party for a relatively obscure politician like myself made me the object of instant envy in Washington—politicians not only have the same fascination with movie stars as everyone else but they're always trying to woo them to their campaigns to cash in on their popularity. So envy fueled the gossip.

I was made crudely aware of all of this by

an alcoholic senator, a fourth-termer from a mid-
west Bible-belt state where public drunkenness
is still a misdemeanor that can land you in jail
—if this senator behaved at home the way he
does in Washington he'd spend half his time in
jail. This particular evening I had gone to a reception at the Iranian Embassy, where the
Shah's wealth has not exactly been stinted to
present a glittery image of his dictatorial re-
gime: the place is overwhelming, and the buf-
fets are always laden with incredible displays
of food, including, of course, the finest golden
caviar. At this bash half official Washington was
there, consuming the booze and food with the
gusto only official Washington can display when
confronted with a groaning board paid for by
somebody else. I was standing in the Persian
Room, a mammoth octagonal reception hall
topped by a thirty-foot-high dome that's a mind-
boggling kaleidoscope of tiny mirrors, all lighted
to shimmer like some huge, inverted cut-glass
bowl. I was talking to a friend of mine, a Mary-
land congressman who's on Banking and Currency with me, when up weaved Senator X, his
eyes glazed, a glass of bourbon clutched in his
claw, his thinning hair rumpled and his puffy
red face amazingly reminiscent of W. C. Fields.
I'd had dealings with the Senator, who pro-
fessed a fondness for me that wasn't returned.
Now he beamed, threw his arm around me, blew
his breath in my face and said, "Bill, old buddy,
I read that *Newsweek* article about your big

party in New York. Goddamn, that must have
been some show. Raised you a lot of money, I
hear?"

"Yes, it certainly helped."

"Helped?" He snorted a laugh. "I hope to
tell you it must have helped! It always helps to
have Big Bucks behind you, and I guess old Bill
here has hit the jackpot in the Big Bucks Sweep-
stake. And goddamn good lookin' she is, too." He
lowered his voice to mezzo forte and gave me a
crude wink. "How is she in the sack, old buddy?
I always had an idea those big-business-women
types would freeze your balls off. True?"

I gave him a look of disgust he was too
drunk to notice. Still, I had to say something.
Senator Loudmouth had brought up what everyone wanted to hear about anyway, and I could
see people moving over, ears cocked.

"Well, you may not believe this, Jerry," I
said (Jerry isn't his name), "but Charlotte
Dreyfus is interested in my politics—"

He whooped. "Your *politics?* Jesus Christ,
what's wrong with you, Bill? Couldn't get it
up?"

"Now look, Jerry, *old buddy*"—I lowered
my voice—"how would it be if I asked how
Waldo Markson was in the sack?" Waldo Markson (again, not the real name) is a fat cat from
Jerry's state who has backed his campaigns from
the beginning. Everyone in Washington also
knows that Jerry does big favors for Waldo
Markson. Jerry's grin vanished.

"Waldo Markson's a fine man," he growled.

"I'm sure you think so, since he's raised about three million for your campaigns. Do you get it up for Waldo?"

"That's a goddamn dirty thing to say!"

"But what you say about me isn't?"

He glared at me, then turned to the congressman I'd been talking to.

"Well, what do *you* think?" he said. "Do you think Charlotte Dreyfus is interested in Bill's politics? First time I ever heard *that* called 'politics.' "

He looked at my midsection, poked my friend in the ribs with his elbow, snorted with laughter and weaved off. A long-suffering public would probably have elected me President if I had strangled him then and there, but I'm against political assassination even when it seems called for. I was also restrained by the fact that I knew this drunken clown had only said what a lot of others were probably thinking.

Later, in my small apartment on Connecticut Avenue, I thought how people were already assuming I was sleeping with Charlotte. Despite what I had said on Julia Ridley's program about the sophistication of the voters, politicians are still judged by different rules, which really is as it' should be. Mr. Average Citizen stumbles, well, it's his business. The President stumbles, it's the world's business. Is he drunk? Clumsy? Dumb? Suffering from some disease they won't talk about? I was hardly in the President's

league, but I had to face the fact that my private
life wasn't run by the same rules as most people's.

I was also becoming aware, though, that my
relationship with Charlotte wasn't the potential
time bomb: Charlotte's money was. Senator X
had been blunt enough about why he thought
I was after Charlotte, and I had no doubt others
would think the same. I even asked myself if
there weren't some truth in the charge. Oh yes,
I was suspicious of the motives of the rich, but
hadn't I also been somewhat dazzled by Charlotte's lifestyle? Yes, but I honestly didn't want
her money. On the contrary—I could tell even
then that her money was going to cause me
nothing but trouble.

Senator X would never have believed it, but
I would have been a lot happier if Charlotte
Dreyfus hadn't had a dime.

The following Tuesday morning I took the
plane to San Francisco, and as luck would have
it I sat next to a man who recognized me. He
was from New York, knew of my campaign and
was a supporter. He was also a doctor, and in
the course of the conversation I took the opportunity to ask him some questions about Nicky's
disease. After all, it had been a little over three
weeks since I had met Charlotte and Nicky at
East Hampton, and according to the macabre
timetable of the disease, Nicky had less than

three weeks to live. Yet at the party she had looked and acted healthy, and I wondered if it might be possible some miracle were happening.

The doctor let me down hard. He told me she would continue to appear healthy almost to the end. But the disease destroyed the blood's ability to clot, and ultimately, although they would continue to give her transfusions, what would probably kill her would be an internal hemorrhage. When I asked him what the normal time span of the disease was, he too said six weeks.

Time was running out.

San Francisco was golden. As the plane landed, the Pacific glinted with reflected sun and the city looked its romantic, gorgeous best. The weather was beautiful and so was the Stanford Court, a new hotel on Nob Hill that was former-ly an apartment building. As I was signing the register I heard a familiar voice behind me say, "You made it!"

I turned to see Nicky. I picked her up and kissed her.

"Of course I made it. How are you?"

"Okay. This is a great hotel and San Fran-cisco's great and Mother's having a business meet-ing till five so will you take me on the Sausalito Ferry?"

It all came out in one breath.

"Will you let me see my room first?"

"All right, but don't take too long, I've got a schedule all drawn up and it's packed." Then she whispered, "Thanks for coming."

I put her down and told her to wait in the lobby. Ten minutes later I was back, and we taxied to the Ferry Building. Nicky seemed strangely subdued. She sat in the cab looking out the window, lost in thought. For such an effervescent child, it was a switch that confused me at first. Then I began to get the feeling that I had misjudged her all along. Or perhaps I had been seeing her one way—as a child—when in reality she was becoming more mature almost by the day. I suppose it was the realization of what was happening to her that was doing it. She, who had been given so much, was having it all jerked away. Being intelligent as well as sensitive, she was jettisoning all the nonessentials of her personality, getting down to the bedrock of will she would need to face the next few weeks. This kid, who I suppose must have struck many people as a wiseass brat, had guts. I not only loved and enjoyed her. Now I was going to come to admire her as well.

I decided to let her do the talking, since obviously something was on her mind. We went to the upper deck of the ferry, which wasn't very crowded. The bay was choppy because of a strong wind, but it was warm and the view was exceptional. We leaned on the rail in silence as the boat chugged out of the slip. Then she said, "I've been feeling pretty guilty this week."

"Why?"

She looked at me, holding on to her hair with one hand to keep it out of her eyes.

"Because I've been pulling a dirty trick on your family. You know: trying to get you and Mother together. It seemed like a terrific idea at first because you'd be so great for her. And I thought if I talked to your son and sort of got his permission, it would be okay. But it really isn't okay, is it? I mean, I've been acting pretty selfish. I guess your wife must hate me."

I thought a moment before answering.

"Let me put it this way, Nicky: if my marriage was perfect, you wouldn't be able to break it up."

She seemed a little relieved.

"Yeah, I suppose." She turned back to look at distant Alcatraz. "Still, it was selfish of me."

"I don't think so. You were thinking of your mother."

"I still am. I worry about her a lot. But . . ."

"What?"

"I don't know. It's just that when I think of everything I've done, it turns out I really haven't done much of anything. I've always thought about *me*. Nicky Dreyfus, the great ballerina. Nicky Dreyfus, the heart-breaker. I've never done much for anybody else, and now it doesn't look like I'm going to have a chance to."

"Hey, come on: you're only eleven. You can't change the world."

She gave me a thoughtful look.

"I might have."

I put my arm around her, and we watched the gulls awhile.

Then I said, "Anyway, as far as Peggy is concerned, she doesn't hate you, and you mustn't feel guilty."

"What are you going to do?"

"I'm not sure."

She hesitated.

"I'm about to be selfish again."

"Okay."

"I'll bet if you asked Mother to marry you, she'd say yes."

I didn't say anything.

"You *do* love her, don't you?" she added, rather anxiously. "I mean, she *is* super-fantastic, don't you think?"

"She's super-fantastic. She may be a little too super-fantastic."

"What's that mean?"

"People are beginning to say things."

She scowled.

"Like *what?*"

"That I'm after your mother's money, for openers."

She groaned.

"How could they be so *dumb?* Mother knows you're not after her money, and if you were she'd be the first to spot it! So tell those creeps to buzz off. God, I could *kill* them!"

"Nicky, people are cynical. When a politician who hasn't got any money leaves his wife to marry a woman whose credit rating is like the Bank of America, they aren't going to say, 'Oh, isn't that wonderful. He *loves* her.' They're going to say, 'Uh huh. That creep's already got his fists on her bank account.' "

"Let 'em say it! So what?"

"So that's not the kind of thing you like to hear about yourself, or somebody you care about."

"Oh, come on. You know you're not like that, so what *difference* does it make what they say? You know you love her." She hesitated, then added nervously, "You *do,* don't you?"

"There are other things besides love—"

"Such as? It's the most important thing in the world, isn't it?"

"You make it all sound so simple."

"Well? It is."

I didn't want to argue with her. Actually, I suspected she was right.

We spent an hour wandering around Sausalito in the sun. I bought her an ice cream cone and a Rock album and . . . well, it sounds banal, I guess, but as I look back on it I remember it as one of the *nicest* afternoons of my life. For a while, I was free of politics, free of worry, and just free. It was delicious.

We took the ferry back and got to the hotel at five-thirty. Nicky took me to the suite she and Charlotte were sharing, which was on the same floor as my room. As we entered I heard water running in the bathroom. Charlotte called out, "Nicky, is that you?"

"Yes." Then she whispered to me, "Don't let her know you're here. Let's surprise her."

"Where have you been?" called Charlotte.

"A sailor picked me up and we made love."

"Seriously."

"I'm serious. He's here now. He's awfully cute, and he's got tattoos in the *weirdest* places."

Charlotte stuck her head out of the bathroom. A towel was wrapped around her hair and she had on a terrycloth bathrobe. When she saw me, she smiled.

"Hi, sailor," she said. "Which weird places do you have tattoos in?"

"He can get in the tub with you and show you!" said Nicky. "It would be a *great* sex scene!"

"Nicky," I said, "why don't you go down to the lobby and ask someone where's a good place for us to have dinner tonight?"

"We've already got a reservation at Jack's."

"Then why don't you go down and buy a paper? In other words, *scram.*"

She sighed. "God, it's awful being a near-adult. All right, I'll give you two a half hour." She went to the door and added, "It's supposed to be *great* in a tub."

And out she went.

"Is it great in a tub?" I asked.

"Want to find out? We've got a half hour till the chaperone returns."

I took off my coat and tossed it on a chair.

"Well, if it lives up to its billing, I'll put it in the *Congressional Record.*"

It wasn't so great. At least, not in that tub. It was too small and I kept slipping and finally Charlotte giggled and said, "Let's just soak, Japanese-style."

"But I'm horny. I didn't come three thousand miles to soak!"

"Wait till tonight. Your room's just down the hall."

"How do you know?"

"I'm a big-time executive, I know how to arrange things."

"You know something?" I said, kissing her sudsy nose. "You're also a sexy big-time executive."

"Mmm . . . why don't you sit at that end, facing me, and we can play toesies and it will be *ravishingly* sensual."

I splashed around like a whale until we were facing each other, and somehow we got our legs arranged. Then I flicked some suds at her and she flicked back, and pretty soon we had the bathroom swamped.

"Now, that's what I call a great sex scene," she said, winked, and we both laughed.

I slid down neck-deep into the warm water. "Nicky says that if I ask you to marry me, you won't say no. Is she right?"

"Nicky has no business saying that, and no,

she's not right. I'd never marry a man who was badgered into asking by my daughter."

"She couldn't badger me. And I'm not asking—at least, now. But I can't afford to fly to California every time I want to take a bath with you."

"I'll grant you that's carrying cleanliness a bit far."

"I love you, Charlotte."

She put her hand on my knee and rubbed it.

"And I love you, my sweet William. You know that. But could you survive a divorce? I mean, politically."

"I think so. I don't know if I could survive marrying you."

"Thanks."

"Politically."

"What's wrong with me?"

"You're too rich."

Suddenly the bathroom was chilly.

"Then don't marry me," she snapped. "You know, you make me feel like some sort of leper because—oh, hell, I don't want to talk about it."

We soaked, and sulked, for a while.

"Well," I finally said, "this is going to be a wonderful three days."

"Isn't it?"

"Shall I take the plane back in the morning?"

She looked sheepish.

"Of course not, dummy. I want you here, you know that. And it's so important for Nicky. . . . What's wrong with having a rich wife?"

She suddenly, and angrily, switched back. "There are a lot of people who think that's not a half-bad idea."

"I'm not a lot of people."

She simmered down.

"I know, but why would it hurt you politically? There are a lot of rich politicians around. Hell, there are hardly any poor ones left."

"They had the money to start with. They didn't leave a wife of eighteen years to marry it, which is what everybody would think of me."

"Then where does that leave us?"

"Sitting in the tub."

She sank down until the water was over her chin.

"Shit," she said.

For some reason, that did it.

"*Will* you marry me?" I said.

She looked surprised. Then, slowly, she came back up out of the water, a smile spreading over her face. "I thought you'd never ask."

I kissed her, and then we got half out of the water and were in each other's arms, our soapy bodies slicking—and you know something?

It is great in a tub.

Well, I had done it. I had popped the question and been accepted, and thereby I had undoubtedly loosed a sea of troubles. But when we told Nicky at dinner it somehow was all worth it. She had planned and, yes, schemed and maneuvered for this moment. And when, after we had been seated at Jack's, I took her hand and said, "Guess what? You're getting a new father," her reaction was special for the occasion. Vintage Nicky would have been an explosion of "supers," "sen-*say*-tionals" and so forth. But now, she was very subdued. She looked at both of us and said quietly, "I love you."

"You know something?" Charlotte said later as we lay in each other's arms in my room. Nicky had already gone to bed.

"What?"

"It's better with you than with anyone else."

"Oh, come on. I know I'm the Great Lover but—"

"No, it's true, Bill. Really."

I kissed her ear. "What can I tell you? I'm Super Lover. By day, a mild-mannered politician. But when I step into a phone booth and—"

"You nut. Anyway, it's true."

We lay there a while. Then she said, "What about Peggy?"

"Let's not think about that for now. Let's just enjoy—"

"We have to think about her. Is the divorce going to be messy?"

"I don't know."

"You feel guilty about her, don't you?"

"Yes and no . . ."

"I wonder if . . ." she began, then stopped.

"If what?"

"I wonder if Nicky hadn't worked so hard to push us together . . . I mean, if it weren't for Nicky, do you think we'd have happened anyway?"

"I don't know. I don't suppose we'll ever know."

"What will happen to us after she's gone?"

I put my hand over her mouth.

"We'll still be us," I told her. "And listen —we've got two more days away from the rest of the world. So we're not going to louse it up by thinking about that. Agreed?"

She nodded. I removed my hand and replaced it with my mouth. I told her, "I love you," and I meant it.

"And I love you, sweet William, more than anybody I've ever known."

Nicky had been right, I decided. It all *did* seem so simple, that warm, wonderful night a continent away from reality. Of course, I was fooling myself about that, but, well, I doubt if many of us could get through life if we didn't fool ourselves some of the time.

Chapter 12

The next morning I rented a car and drove us all down to Carmel for lunch (Carmel for lunch was part of Nicky's schedule). The good weather held up and I was in high spirits, as was Nicky. Charlotte, for some reason, seemed down. Or perhaps "groggy" was the word. I suppose I should have realized that with what she was going through, she might have been taking something to help her. We poked around Carmel for a while, then went to lunch. The weather was unbelievably lovely. I ordered a bottle of good California white wine to go with the abalone and was rather surprised how fast it vanished down Charlotte's throat, as well as how quickly the alcohol affected her. She seemed to levitate into a blissful haze that lasted halfway back to San Francisco. I didn't give it too much thought, but that night she repeated her performance con brio. At six we went to the Cannery, the red-brick, nineteenth-century factory that clever architects have converted into a combination shopping-center-arcade. The three of us browsed around, then went to nearby Fisherman's Wharf for dinner. This time Charlotte pulled out all the stops. She ordered champagne before the meal, and during the meal downed another bottle of wine.

"Hadn't you better take it a little easy?" I asked as she ordered a second bottle.

"Why? It's a vacation, isn't it? And when I'm in California I like to sample the local wines. They never ship the good stuff to New York."

"You don't have to drink up the whole state."

She gave me a haughty look.

"I'm just having a few glasses," she said grandly.

Came the second bottle, and by dessert she was swaying in her chair, her eyelids at half-mast. Nicky was watching her too. Now she whispered to me, "I think Mother's bombed out of her skull."

"No kidding. Let's get some coffee down her, then float her back to the hotel."

I signaled the waiter, who brought and poured coffee. Charlotte tried some, which served to wake her out of her daze. She burped and smiled at us, blearily.

"Everybody having fun?" she slurred. "*I* am. Having the most wonderful time."

Nicky rolled her eyes.

"She's too *much*," she whispered.

"We'd better get her to bed."

"Our room or yours?"

Good old practical Nicky.

"Yours."

"Okay." She took her mother's hand. "It's time to go," she said. "I'm pooped."

Charlotte looked at her daughter and smiled.

"Did I ever tell you you're beautiful?" she said. "Did I ever tell you how precious you are to me?"

Nickly looked embarrassed, and a bit tense.

"I know that, Mother. Come on."

"*Did* I tell you?" she persisted. "Because you *are* precious to me. Most precious thing in the whole world."

Nicky shot me a helpless look.

"Come on, Charlotte, let's get out of here."

"Oh, let's stay. I like this place. I like fish. *You* must like fish, you're Norwegian."

"I love fish but let's go . . ."

"Look!" She took a rose from the vase on the table and held it to her head. "Carmen! Wanna see me do the Habañera? I'm a great Carmen!"

"Right, and I'm a dynamite Don José. But let's go back to the hotel . . ."

"No, I wanna dance."

Before I could stop her, she put the rose between her teeth, rolled out of her chair and began clapping her hands over her head. Flamenco-style.

"Mother!" groaned Nicky.

Useless. Taking the rose out of her mouth, Charlotte started singing the Habañera, dancing around the adjacent tables as the other diners stared.

> *"L'amour est un oiseau rebelle*
> *Que nul ne peut apprivoiser,*
> *Et c'est bien en vain qu'on l'appelle,*
> *S'il lui convient de refuser . . .*

I was out of my seat, after her.

> *"Rien n'y fait, menace ou prière*
> *L'un parle bien l'autre se taît;*
> *Et c'est l'autre que je préfère*
> *Il n'a rien dit, mais il me plaît.*
> *L'amour . . ."*

She had just hit the "L'a-moooor" when I grabbed her arm. Undaunted, she gave forth with the second "L'amoooor," then the third and fourth as the restaurant rocked with laughter. As she finished she threw her rose in the air, and everyone applauded. Beaming, she took a bow, then looked at me.

"How was that?" she said. "Wasn't I great? See, I *am* talented. Wanna hear me do the 'Anvil Chorus'?"

"No, we're going."

We started toward the door, Charlotte blowing kisses to her new fans, Nicky in tow. When we got outside she grinned at me.

"You're mad," she giggled.

"No. As a matter of fact, you're pretty good."

"Good? I'm sensational!" At which point, she started swaying, and I caught her in my arms.

"Get a cab," I told Nicky.

By the time we got back to her hotel room she was out on her feet. I plopped her across the bed as Nicky took off her shoes.

"Does she do this often?" I asked.

"The last time was when she divorced my father. I told you she's not as tough as you think." She stopped. She looked frightened. "You know, she's on Valium. She got her doctor to get her some before we left New York. Valium and wine is a bad news combination. That's why she's so zonked."

"Where does she keep it?"

"In the bathroom. Want me to get it?"

"Yes."

She ran into the bathroom and reappeared a moment later with a bottle of pills.

"I'll keep them," I said, taking the bottle from her and putting it in my pocket. I went over to the bed, leaned down and kissed Charlotte's hair. She was lying on her stomach, her face half buried in the pillow.

When I straightened, I saw Nicky watching me.

"I made the right choice, didn't I?" she said quietly. "You're going to take good care of her."

"I'm going to try."

I think she knew I meant it.

Charlotte's bravura performance wasn't helping matters, and the next morning I went back to her suite to straighten her out—or at least to try. When she opened the door I saw she was wearing a bathrobe, and, by Charlotte's standards, she looked a wreck.

"How are you?" I asked, coming inside.

"I feel like the entire Second World War was fought on my tongue," she groaned. "What happened? The last thing I remember, I've forgotten."

"You got drunk."

"So I gather."

I followed her into the suite.

"Where's Nicky?"

"Downstairs getting me some aspirin. I hope you're not going to give me a sermon?"

"You realize you're making things tougher for her?"

She turned on me.

"I can't help it! Do you realize what it's like watching her every day, knowing that damned *thing* inside her is eating away at her, killing her by inches..."

"We all realize that! But getting drunk doesn't help, and taking Valium sure as *hell* doesn't help!"

"Then what *does* help? That's what's so obscene about this. We can't *do* anything. We just have to stand and watch..."

She was crying now and I took her by the arms. "Goddammit," I said, "stop it, Charlotte. Do you want her seeing you this way? I understand how you feel, but the worst thing we can do is come apart at the seams when Nicky needs all the support she can possibly get."

"I know . . . but I had so many plans for her..."

"You've *got* to stop thinking this way!"

"But I *can't!*" I let her go, and she sank down on the edge of the bed. Finally she said, "Nicky's the only one. I can't have any more children."

"Why not?"

"Three years ago, I had a hysterectomy. There was a cyst . . . it turned out to be benign but they were worried and they recommended taking everything out. I went along . . . doctor knows best . . . except I wonder . . ." She looked up. "I'd love to have had a child with you. The other night, I was thinking about that and about you, and I couldn't get to sleep. That's when I hit the Valiums." She hesitated, then added, "Do you have them?"

"Yes, and I'm keeping them. You don't need pills to get through this."

She reached out her hand and held mine.

"I need *you*," she said. Finally she sighed and stood up. "All right, I've had my cry. I've been telling myself all along there weren't going to be any tears. Easier to say . . ."

"I know."

"It won't happen again. Tonight's our last night here. We've got to make it special for her. The ballet, the whole number . . ." She forced a smile. "I guess it wouldn't look too good if I fell on my ass."

"Just don't get on the stage and sing the 'Habañera.' "

"Did I do *that?*"

"You did. In the restaurant. It was a memorable performance."

"My God." She started laughing as she headed for the bathroom. "Well, leave it to me. When I make an ass of myself, I don't do it half way. Oh Charlotte, you *jerk*."

And she vanished into the john.

It was hard for both of us, trying to give Nicky the time of her life when we knew it was probably the last time . . . Nicky was remarkable. Somehow, through some extraordinary act of will, she seemed to have made her peace with her "shitty" deal. But even she began to show the strain that night at the ballet. It was, for her, the highlight of the trip, and all through the day she became increasingly wound up as curtain time approached. We had a light supper, then went up to change. Twenty minutes later I went to their room and knocked. Charlotte opened the door. "Sen-*say*-tional," I said as I took in the pink chiffon evening dress, the diamonds and emeralds.

"Tonight has to be magic," she said.

Nicky was still in her bedroom. Five minutes later she came out in a yellow dress.

"I've got the two most beautiful women in San Francisco," I said.

They both smiled and nodded.

We taxied to the opera house, where an elegant-looking crowd was making its way in for the performance. Several photographers were taking pictures, and the sight of them gave me a moment of panic. Nobody knew me in San Francisco, but Charlotte's face was well-known. Suppose one of them took a picture of us and it was picked up by a wire service? I then promptly told myself that was unlikely—besides, I wasn't about to spoil the evening. Of course, as we went in our picture was taken. When I saw the raised camera I looked the other way, but I had no idea whether I'd looked far enough.

"Don't worry," whispered Charlotte, who caught what I'd done. "It's just for the local papers."

I know little about ballet, so all I can say is that the dancers from Russia seemed to me incredible and the dancing beautiful, which isn't saying much, or perhaps says everything. The program was "Swan Lake" and the prima ballerina was the great Soviet star Ekaterina Maximova. Because the Bolshoi's appearances in America are rare, the audience was especially keyed up. I thought of Nicky's Tchaikovsky T-shirt and the taped-up poster of Pavlova in her practice room. I looked at her, sitting between her mother and me. She was staring at the curtain, waiting for the performance to begin, and she looked unusually serious, as if she were attending a mystic rite. Then the houselights lowered, the wonderful music began, the curtain raised, and we were in the Prince's castle.

Nicky never fidgeted, never moved. She watched with total absorption. When Maximova did her famous thirty-two *fouettés*, I heard her gasp softly with admiration. When the performance was over and the audience rose to cheer, she continued to sit in her seat, motionless. I looked down at her face and saw, for the first time, her remarkable composure cracking. Tears were streaming down her face as she stared at the performers.

Chapter
13

I suppose into every politician's career there comes a moment when he secretly curses the invention of the photograph. Before the daguerreotype the majority of the human race had only a hazy idea of what their leaders looked like. Reproductions of idealized state portraits, painted by paid-to-flatter artists, turned dumpy, uninspiring royalty, presidents and congressmen into what must have seemed near-gods. Well, the camera did away with that. Politicians are no longer near-gods. The problem is, now we're all too human.

The morning after the ballet I took an early plane back to New York (Charlotte and Nicky were taking a following one), arriving at Kennedy late in the afternoon, New York time. My plan was to go home to West Schuyler and tell Peggy my decision about Charlotte and me. When I bought the *Post* at the airport newsstand I saw part of my news had already been broken. There, on page three, filling half the page, was the photo of the three of us going into the San Francisco Opera House. As I had feared, it must have been grabbed up by an eager editor when he saw it on the wire service. My face, half turned from the camera, was still recognizable. The caption read: "A Mercedes in Dalton's Pot?" And, underneath, "Congressman William Dalton, a contender for New York's Democratic senatorial nomination, was photographed last night entering the San Francisco Opera House with Cosmetic Queen Charlotte Dreyfus and her daughter. Miss Dreyfus, a multimillionairess, recently gave a thousand dollar a plate fund-raising party for Congressman Dalton at her lavish Fifth Avenue triplex. Dalton's Minimum Income scheme, recently outlined in a Harlem speech, promised 'A Mercedes in every pot.' Looks like the congressman got there first."

That was all, and it was enough. I went to a phone booth and called Tony Gleason at his Brooklyn Heights home. When he answered I said, "It's Bill. I've seen the *Post*."

"So have I. What's your position on suicide?"

"Funny. Meet me at the Dorset in an hour. Bring Herb Ross. I've got to make a statement."

"What will you say? Those California bankers you were addressing just happened to look like Charlotte Dreyfus . . . ?"

"Cut the shit!" I said, and slammed down the phone. An hour later the three of us were together in the hotel, Tony and Herb on the sofa watching me as I paced about the room.

"All right," I said, "I know it looks bad, but it's not as bad as it looks."

"Wonderful," said Tony. "Tell us the good news."

"I'm marrying Charlotte."

Tony and Herb exchanged looks.

"That's good news?" said Tony.

"Yes. And I know people are going to think I'm after her money—hell, they already think it —but I *love* her. And that's the statement I'm going to make."

"You're going to marry the woman you love," said Tony, lighting a Cigarillo. "You're going to divorce your nice, schleppediche wife of eighteen years and marry the woman you love who's worth a hundred million clams on the hoof. Sounds like a nightmare re-run of the Duke of Windsor, with the roles reversed."

"I don't care what it sounds like. Charlotte and I are going to get married. Now what the hell is so un-American about that?"

"Everything's wrong with it, and you know it. Hell, you're better off screwing her in California and getting caught—at least that makes you sort of sympathetic in a macho way. 'Vote for Dalton, the X-Rated Senator.' But *marry* her? The voters would never forgive you. People don't like sell-outs, and you marrying Charlotte Dreyfus is a sell-out."

"To what?"

"To money! The Establishment! To the Fat Cats! Forget it, Bill. My advice is, don't say anything. Or just say you ran into her in San Francisco and went to the opera with her. Big deal."

"It was the ballet."

"Same thing. So people will talk, but it's a long way till the election, and chances are most of them will forget it after a month or so. But *marry* her? My God . . . sure, do it if you want to. But forget the Senate. I doubt if you'd even hang onto your House seat. The folks in Apple Country aren't going to like being represented by Mr. Charlotte Dreyfus."

I tried to control my temper.

"Tony, that's going too damn far. I'm Bill Dalton, I'm a congressman . . . just because I marry a rich woman doesn't mean I suddenly become her lapdog, for God's sake!"

"Doesn't it?"

"No!"

He shrugged. "Okay, then do it. Herb, write him a statement. Stick in 'marrying the woman

I love.' Maybe put in the lapdog bit—don't use that word, but something close, like 'toady' or 'minion.' But keep emphasizing the 'love' angle, because all the world loves a lover—right? Then we'll call the media boys and arrange a press conference. It should be good for a few laughs. Ten in the morning okay, Bill?"

They were both looking at me. I rubbed my forehead, trying to think. Finally I said, "Don't write it, Herb. And don't call a press conference."

"You want to just issue a statement?"

"No, I want to *think!*"

"That'll be a refreshing change," said Tony, getting up from the sofa. "Okay, I'm going back home. Call me if you have any more brainstorms. Herb, you coming?"

"Do you want me to stick around, Bill?"

I shook my head. "No, go on."

Herb is a nice kid, nowhere near as hard-boiled as Tony. Now he said, rather awkwardly, "I'm sorry, Bill. But I think Tony's right."

"Maybe he is. I don't know. Thanks."

"Well, good night."

"Good night."

They left the room. I stared out the window and wondered what in God's name to do. I thought of Peggy. It was bad enough knowing your husband was in California with another woman, but to have it plastered all over the newspapers? That was a gratuitous twist of the knife. And Charlotte. Her face was in that picture too. She had a career, and while it wasn't dependent on the whims of the voters as mine was, I doubted she'd be too happy when she read the *Post* caption. I knew her plane was due at Kennedy at eight so I decided to grab a hamburger, then go to her apartment building and wait for her. I went downstairs and walked uptown, then over to Madison Avenue. I spotted a small hamburger place and went in to sit at the counter. There were a half dozen other customers, but fortunately no one recognized me, although one woman in a booth was reading, God help me, the *Post*. Empathizing with hunted criminals, I ordered a hamburger and a Coke and tried to make myself as inconspicuous as possible. For ten minutes all went well. Then, just as I was biting into my burger, things started to go to hell.

A shopping-bag lady came into the hamburger stand. For those of you who don't know some of the more bizarre aspects of New York City, I'll explain that shopping-bag ladies are pathetic older women who live on the streets. They carry all their worldly possessions with them in shopping bags, and how they survive it's hard to imagine. But they do, and they can be found in any neighborhood. This particular shopping-bag lady favored Madison Avenue, and apparently Fate had fingered her to be my personal Nemesis. She immediately spotted me.

"Look who's here!" said she in a loud voice, pointing. "It's Lover-Boy Dalton!"

I turned to stare. She was enormous, her

girth padded by three or four ragged coats. She had some sort of beach hat scrunched on her head, and her feet were squeezed into a pair of ancient tennis shoes. She had set down her half dozen D'Agostino shopping bags, which were loaded with junk. She looked more than a little crazy. Now the other customers were staring at me, the woman in the booth checking her *Post* to match up my face and the photo.

Ms. Shopping Bag commenced to cackle. "Well, he's cute," she said, addressing no one and everyone. "I can see why Miss Rich Bitch goes for him. But wouldn't you think *one* politician could keep his pants on? Just *one?* They're all the same, every one of them. Starting with Calvin Coolidge. I ought to know, I was his mistress."

She said this so matter-of-factly it brought a few titters, but most of the others were frozen. Some, I think, were embarrassed for me, all were fascinated by this impromptu one-woman performance by Cal Coolidge's self-proclaimed ex-mistress. She sat down on a counter stool. I noticed the counterman, a young Puerto Rican, grinning broadly at me, obviously pleased by my discomfort. Why not?

"Coolidge was a dirty old man," went on Ms. D'Ag Bag. "All he thought about was sex. That's why they called him Silent Cal, he was always thinking about girls! Bet you didn't know *that*. Well, there's lot of things I could tell you about politicians, starting with *this* one right here," and she stabbed her finger in my direction. I was immobile, staring at her as if she were a cobra. "I wouldn't vote for you," she went on, addressing me now directly. "You know why? It's not because you got caught with that rich bitch. And it's not because you're probably on the take. *All* you politicians are on the take. You really want to know why I wouldn't vote for you?"

Silence. All eyes turned on me.

"Why?" I said, trapped.

"Because you've got three nipples! All politicians have three nipples! Cal Coolidge did. That's the Mark of the Devil, the third nipple, and all politicians are children of Satan!"

Now she was howling with laughter. Everyone started laughing. I don't know, it was all so crazy, and though I momentarily considered saying something in defense of my profession, I finally started laughing too. Feeling punchy, I finally got off the stool, paid my check and left the hamburger stand. Everyone else was still laughing, including the counterman. It was crazy. New York is crazy. I went out onto Madison Avenue and leaned against the side of the building until I could collect myself. Crazy.

I had heard the Voice of the Voter. The voter thought all politicians were children of Satan. Well, who knows ... ?

After a while, when I had calmed down, I started walking towards Charlotte's, and then it didn't seem quite so funny anymore. The opinion of the Shopping Bag Lady, the cynical caption in the *Post*, Tony's voter-tabulator-eye view of my position was probably a better reading of what the public was actually thinking about me than what the best and most expensive poll could produce. Well, I shouldn't have been surprised. I had known there would be problems if I married Charlotte. But knowing something is not the same as being jolted by the actual event, and the picture in the paper and the encounter with the Voice of the Voter had been, to me, jarringly real.

Money. It was almost laughably ironic that money was finally the villain. Charlotte's millions. Money makes the world go round, money talks, money is the root of all evil—the hundreds of clichés about money that abound in our language are probably as good evidence as there is of the enormous influence it has over our lives, whether we like to admit it or not. Most people's lives are blighted by lack of it. My weird problem was that my life was being thrown out of kilter by an abundance of it—or, at least, Charlotte's abundance. An ironic problem for the noble voice of the oppressed—but damn it, an honest problem nonetheless.

All of which ignored one glaring point: I wasn't interested in money, I was interested in being a senator. Politicians might be children of Satan, but politics was in my blood.

Money. By the time I reached Charlotte's building I was hating it with a passion.

I saw the car as I turned the corner onto Fifth Avenue. An innocent-looking gray Buick, it was parked across from Charlotte's apartment building. The only noteworthy thing about it was that it was parked illegally, but I wasn't a traffic cop. I went into the building, to be shuttled aside by Charlie Simmons, who was on duty that night. "Reporters," he said, pointing at the Buick. "They've been here for an hour waiting to see Miss Dreyfus when she gets in from the airport."

Now I saw two men getting out of the car. They hurried across the street.

"They must have spotted me," I said.

"Do you want to talk to them?"

"Not now. But you can tell them I'll be down later. Is Miss Dreyfus in?"

"Clyde's picking her up at Kennedy. The manager's got the key to the apartment but he's out. Would you mind waiting here?" He pointed to the north end of the big T-shaped lobby, and I went around the corner as Charlie delivered my message to the reporters.

Fifteen minutes passed as I sat at the end of the lobby, steaming. Periodically Charlie would come around to report that they were still waiting. Then he would return to his post at the door. I couldn't leave the building without running into them, which I didn't want to do without first talking to Charlotte.

Finally I heard Charlie open the door. Voices came in from the street. I looked around the corner to see a maroon Rolls-Royce limousine parked at the curb. Clyde, dressed in a chauffeur's uniform, was arguing with the reporters while Nicky and Charlotte hurried into the building. They saw me and came over, out of sight of the street.

"Scandal!" said Nicky excitedly. "Did you see the *Post?* I'm a star!"

"Nicky, be quiet," said her mother.

She paid no attention.

"Why don't you go out and talk to them? Tell them we were all in San Francisco together and so *what?*"

"It's not that simple, Super-Brat."

"Why? Tell them you and Mother are going to get married. *That's* simple. Want me to tell them?

"No!" I got it out so quickly Charlotte gave me a startled look.

"Maybe we're *not* getting married?" she said.

"What do you mean?" Nicky glared at me. "It's all set! Don't tell me you're backing out?"

This, accusingly. Well, I thought—the hour of decision. I looked at Nicky, her face so suddenly concerned as she sensed the special world she had so painstakingly constructed was beginning to crack. I looked at Charlotte, so lovely and desirable, so loved. So goddamn rich. I thought of lapdogs, I thought of the Senate, I thought of Peggy. The billions of neurons in my head flashed and whirred, circuits broke, and the whole complex machine almost went tilt. Finally I took both their hands.

"Come on," I said. "Let's go out and *tell* them."

We started toward the door.

"*What* are we telling them?" asked Nicky.

"That we're one big happy family and why shouldn't we go to the ballet in San Francisco if we want to?"

She flashed the biggest smile of her life.

"*That's* more like it!"

Outside the reporters and Clyde were still going at each other, but when they saw the three of us emerge from the building the reporters broke off negotiations with Clyde and turned on us. They were both young, and one had a camera that he now used to take our picture. I smiled as agreeably as I could.

"Good evening, gentlemen. I understand you'd like to talk with me?"

"We sure would, congressman," said the one without the camera. "Were you hiding from us?"

"I was waiting for Miss Dreyfus so we could talk to you together. Any objections to that?"

"No sir. We're glad you're cooperating. I'm Phil Stern of U.P. and this is George Hayes. We wondered if you had any comment about that picture in today's *Post?*"

I shrugged. "The three of us attended the ballet last evening in San Francisco. There's no law against that, is there? I didn't break into the Democratic National Headquarters."

"That's right, congressman. The *Post* seems to think you broke into the Treasury instead." He grinned at Charlotte, and I felt my temper uncoiling. "Do you have any comment on the caption? You know, 'A Mercedes in Dalton's Pot'?"

"I suppose something like that's to be expected. It makes for headlines. The fact is Miss Dreyfus and I intend to be married."

"Oh, you're getting married? Congratulations."

"Thanks."

He turned to Charlotte. "Are you looking forward to being a politician's wife, Miss Dreyfus?"

She smiled. "Very much. Particularly *this* politician's."

"Will you be helping in his campaign? Financially, for example?"

Charlotte looked at me uncertainly.

"We haven't discussed that," she said.

"You already *have* helped him, so it's reasonable to assume—"

"She *said*, we haven't discussed it," I interrupted. I felt he was really pushing it.

He turned back to me. "But with campaign financing so difficult these days, you wouldn't object to Miss Dreyfus helping you. Correct, congressman?"

"As a matter of fact, I probably would. I've always financed my campaigns on my own and I'll continue to."

He looked skeptical. "But Miss Dreyfus *has* already helped you . . ."

"She gave a party. If she wants to give more parties when she's my wife, I'll be happy to go to them. Thank you and good night."

I turned, signaling to Charlotte and Nicky to go back into the building. We were almost at the door when I heard Stern say, "Congressman, you don't see any conflict between your plan to put an income floor under the poor and your marrying Miss Dreyfus?"

I should have ignored him. Instead I turned back and said, "No one said that to the Kennedys, for example, so why should the rules change for me or anybody else? I want to eliminate poverty. You gentlemen seem to want to eliminate wealth. There's a difference."

"I don't want to eliminate it, just spread it around. Like you're doing, Miss Dreyfus."

"What do you mean by that?" said Charlotte.

"Well, by marrying the congressman you're spreading the wealth, wouldn't you say? Or will you keep separate bank accounts?"

He grinned. I burned. I came back to him and said, "Look—I don't mind what you say about me, but I want you to leave Miss Dreyfus out of this. Okay?"

"I just asked a question—"

"And it was a loaded one. Now, just lay off."

But he didn't. He looked past me to Charlotte.

"Miss Dreyfus, will you campaign with the congressman?"

"The interview is *over* . . ."

Charlotte put her hand on my arm. "Bill, calm down."

"I'm calm!"

She addressed Stern. "I probably will do some campaigning if Bill wants me to," she said.

"Do you think your marrying the congressman will help sell your cosmetics?"

I was dumbfounded. "What the *hell* kind of a question is that?"

"A legitimate one." He shrugged.

"I told you to leave her out of this . . ."

"Look, congressman, our readers are interested in you and Miss Dreyfus. A lot of our female readers use Miss Dreyfus' lipstick—probably some of the men too . . . they want to know about your marriage." He turned back to Charlotte. "Your two previous marriages ended in divorce, didn't they, Miss Dreyfus?"

Now Charlotte looked surprised.

"Yes . . ."

"Do you think politicians make better husbands than, say, stockbrokers and novelists?"

"That's *it*," I said. "No more questions."

I started back into the building, shepherding Charlotte and Nicky in front of me, and I heard Stern say, "What about your present wife, congressman? How's she taking this?"

"No comment."

"She must have some interesting ideas about what kind of a husband politicians make."

I was almost through the door, but that stopped me. Again I turned and glared at him.

"Bill," whispered Charlotte, "come inside."

"This guy has insulted you, me, Peggy—"

"He's needling you, darling. Don't let him, *please*."

Stern was watching us. "Sorry if I upset you, congressman. Just doing my job."

"Have *you* ever been divorced?" I asked, advancing on him.

Now it was his turn to look surprised.

"Well ... yes ... but I don't think that—"

"And how did your first wife take it?"

"She . . . that's none of your business. You're the public figure, not me."

"Oh, come on. I'm just a curious citizen. Have you remarried? Got a girl?"

"Look, congressman, no one's interested in *my* sex life, but plenty of people are interested in yours—which, I might add, seems to be pretty active ..."

And he grinned at Charlotte.

"You know something?" I was standing in front of him. "You're a wise-ass son of a bitch."

"Can I quote you?" He smiled.

Now that I look back on it, I think it was the smile that got to me. It was so damned snide. At any rate my temper had reached the critical mass. I belted him. Right in the smile. He sprawled backward over the rear of the Rolls and stumbled into the street. His partner immediately raised his camera and I jumped him. I heard Charlotte call out, "Bill *don't!*" Just as I wrenched the camera away from Hayes I felt Stern grab my ankle and jerk it from under me. I lost my balance and fell, Hayes's camera in my hands. I saw the rear fender of the Rolls sailing up to my face. I tried to throw up my arm. Too late. It hit my forehead, and everything went black.

Congressman Dalton was knocked cold by a Rolls-Royce.

Chapter
14

They took me to Doctors' Hospital in an ambulance, but it turned out they were over-reacting. It was just a crack on the head, not a concussion, but I guess when doctors get their hands on you they can't resist fussing (or maybe running up a bill). Anyway, they put me in a private room for the night and told me they would x-ray my skull in the morning. I was too tired and my head hurt too much to argue. The nurse gave me something for the pain, and I quickly fell asleep. My last thought was that I would wake up an ex-politician.

They took the x-rays before breakfast, then I was brought back to my room and given a tray. I ate the cold egg and soggy toast, then got in bed with my coffee, the *Times* and the *News*. "Dalton Decks Reporter" was the headline in the *News*, which had it on the fourth page. The *Times* had put it on the entertainment page between porno-movie ads (maybe the *Times* was trying to tell me something). Both pages printed most of the interview and then described the fight. Since I had broken Hayes's camera, I was at least spared a picture.

I had just finished the papers when the door to my room opened. There was Charlotte. I will never forget how she looked, because she had never seemed more beautiful and, at the same time, more distant. She was wearing a sort of silvery blue suit, and she looked like an ice princess out of some Norwegian saga. She also looked ice-cold. Something clearly was wrong. She came into the room, closed the door and said in crisp tones, "I knew you were a hick, congressman, but I never thought you were also a stupid one."

Not exactly the words of a woman in love. I looked at her in disbelief.

"Good morning to you too," I mumbled.

She came to the side of the bed. I was amazed—she was really furious.

"How *could* you have done such a moronic thing? Attacking that reporter—God! And right in front of my building . . . don't you realize you've not only made a fool of yourself, but of me and my daughter?"

"You might ask how my head feels."

"I don't give a damn. You've made me look like the biggest idiot in the world! 'Charlotte Dreyfus, The "Other" Woman with the Battling Congressman' . . . I could kill you. I could absolutely kill you."

"Look, I'm sorry, but that creep got to me—"

"You *let* him get to you! Don't you know anything about how to handle reporters? What have you been doing for eight years? God, I shouldn't ask. You've been talking to the West Carrotville Bugle, or whatever the hell's the name of that burg you come from. Well, this is New York City, and around here you *don't* punch reporters!"

"I said I'm sorry . . ."

"When I think of all the trouble I took to get you into the big leagues, introducing you to people who could really help you. . . . Do you think they'd even talk to you now? I'll be lucky if they talk to *me!*"

I was dumbfounded. It was like seeing and hearing a totally different woman.

"Now, wait a minute, Charlotte. I didn't *ask* you to introduce me to anyone—"

"I'm so damned stupid to have put my faith in you, to believe you had a chance to be a senator—"

"Would you knock this off? I've apologized

about last night. I let my temper get out of control and I'm sorry—for the third time. But the last thing I need is you ranting and raving at me—"

"I'm not going to rant or rave. Frankly, you're not worth a rant, and you sure as hell aren't worth a rave. I'm only here to tell you personally what I think of you, and that I want you to call the papers and retract that ridiculous statement."

"What ridiculous statement?"

"That you and I are getting married. Do you think I intend to be the wife of a two-bit upstate lawyer going nowhere? And believe me, that's where you're going after last night's fiasco."

I stared at her.

"Then all that talk about love . . ."

"Sex in a bathtub. Period."

So much for love.

"I guess I *am* stupid . . ."

"You said it, congressman. Not I."

She went to the door and opened it.

"Charlotte . . ."

She turned to look at me.

"Say good-by to Nicky for me, will you?"

"Yes."

"Thanks. And thanks for taking off the funny face before it was too late."

She frowned, and for a moment I thought I saw—what? Regret, perhaps? Or was I just imagining it? Whatever the look was, it vanished as fast as it had appeared, replaced once more by the ice-mask. She went out, closing the door behind her.

Well, what can I say? I was stunned? Completely thrown might come closer. I didn't want to believe this woman was the same Charlotte I'd known. I didn't want to believe I was such a rotten judge of character to have been taken in so completely. It had been just what it was—a performance. But if it had been, it was a superb one. And what was the point of it?

No, I had to conclude I had seen the real Charlotte Dreyfus, and it wasn't a pretty picture. I felt angry, bitter, hurt and stupid.

Also suddenly very alone.

Just how alone was to become clear that afternoon. I got out of the hospital with a clean bill of health and called Tony Gleason.

"Well, you can forget one worry," I said. "I'm not marrying Charlotte Dreyfus."

"*That's* good news. What happened?"

"She let me have it this morning with both barrels. They're still smoking. I'm through with *that* . . . well, to hell with it. I'm through with her. Is there anything left of my campaign, or do I start looking for gainful employment?"

There was a long silence. Finally he said, "Are you willing to quit the horsing around and start working?"

"Yes."

"Then there's something left of your campaign, now that she's out of the picture. I've talked to Phil Stern. He's not exactly your number one fan but he's not going to sue, thank God. Pay Hayes for his camera and they'll let bygones be bygones. I think, though, that we've got to make a statement about you and Miss Face Cream."

"Sure . . . okay, go ahead . . . make it loud and clear. Say I never want to see her again! Say her face cream makes wrinkles."

"Right, I'll handle it. You'd better get home and start trying to patch things up with Peggy. Then I'd go away for a while and lie low. Take a vacation for ten days. Go where the reporters can't find you. If you can't see 'em you can't hit 'em."

"You've got a point. There's a cabin on a lake near West Schuyler that belongs to a friend of mine. No phone, no electricity, no nothing. I can go there."

"Perfect. Go fish, or whatever. Then call me in ten days and we'll start over. I'm sorry you had to find out about your Charlotte the hard way, but maybe it's just as well."

"Yeah, I guess."

"Well, like they say, love is blind. Have fun at the lake, and good luck with Peggy. You'll need it."

I hung up, still numb. Charlotte, Charlotte. It still seemed inconceivable . . . I still remembered that momentary look as she was leaving the hospital room. I wanted to cling to it, to convince myself it meant what I wanted it to mean.

I tried, and I couldn't.

I flew to West Schuyler and got to our house in midafternoon. It was a chilly, gusty day, and already the maple leaves were turning red. Summer was over.

Jeff was in the driveway, shooting baskets. When he saw my car he stopped and watched me. I was apprehensive about Peggy, but I was also a little apprehensive about Jeff. Despite what he had said to me at Charlotte's party, his life *had* gotten involved—it was his father who had hit the reporter and made a damn fool of himself. His one-time hero had turned into a buffoon, and I wondered if his friends were already laughing at him. I got out of the car and came over to him. "Did you see the papers?"

"Hard to miss them." He smiled. "You really matted that reporter, didn't you?"

"I guess so. It wasn't too smart." I looked at him a moment. "Things still okay between us? I wouldn't blame you if they weren't—"

"Are you kidding?"

"I'm very serious."

"Hey, dad—this is Jeff, remember?"

I put my arm around him and said a heartfelt "Thanks," then added, "How's your mother?"

"I don't think she's going to ask for your autograph... How's Nicky?"

Yes, Nicky. In my anger I hadn't really

thought about her. What a letdown it was going to be for her. All her careful maneuvering...

"Well," I said, "she seemed to have a great time in San Francisco."

"Is she still ... I mean, is there any change?"

"No change."

He frowned.

"What about you and her mother?"

"*There* there definitely has been a change."

I took the ball from him, tried a set shot and missed. I shrugged. "Win a few, lose a few."

I went into the kitchen. Peggy was on the phone, apparently talking to a customer. When she saw me, her face registered nothing. She didn't even interrupt the conversation. I might have been the Invisible Man. I got a Tab from the refrigerator and waited for her to hang up. When she did she said, "Well, I guess I don't have to ask how things were in San Francisco."

"No, you don't."

"And the brawl with the reporters. So dignified, Bill. Just what we all expect from a senator."

"Okay, Peggy, you're entitled. It was hardly the way to announce to you my plans for divorce and remarriage. Except, if it's any interest to you, it's all off."

"Oh? Trouble in paradise? Did the lady lose faith in her candidate?"

"I guess you could put it that way."

"And now the vanquished is home from the

hills, licking his wounds and, I suppose, expecting a patient and loving wife to take him back in her arms..."

"I'm not sure what I'm expecting."

She cut me off with a wave of her hand and got out of her chair. "Come on," she said, "I want to show you something. We can take my car."

"What are you going to show me?"

"A house."

"Peggy, what the hell is this? I'm trying to talk about our marriage and suddenly you're going to sell me a house?"

She was at the back door.

"Just let *me* do the talking, Bill. Come on."

I finished the Tab and followed her to her car. She got in the driver's seat, I in the death seat (apt) and, after telling Jeff we'd be back in a half hour, she started out of town. We drove in silence for a while, then she said, "How's the little girl?"

"Nicky? Not so good. She doesn't have much more time."

"I shouldn't have taken offense at her that night at the party. I can hardly blame her for taking sides. She was the matchmaker, wasn't she?"

"Yes. Some match."

She said nothing more, and soon we turned into a weeded drive. We bumped over the rutted

dirt road heading for a distant farmhouse. The
drive bisected a hilly field that looked as if it
hadn't been tended for years. As we neared the
house I could see it hadn't been tended for generations. Sagging roofline, peeling paint, chim-
neys in need of pointing, broken windows, empty
beer bottles and trash strewn around the over-
grown yard: the place was a derelict, though the
house must have once been a Colonial gem.

Peggy parked the car.

"What is this, Wuthering Heights?"

"It's my new home."

She got out and started toward the porch.

"What does that mean?"

"It came on the market while you were in
San Francisco. Some developer from Utica
wanted to buy the farm and turn it into a trailer
camp—imagine, this gorgeous land a trailer
camp? So I outbid him and bought it. Twenty
acres and the house for thirty-two thousand. Believe me, that's not a bad buy. Watch the porch,
most of the planks are rotten."

She pushed open the front door and went
into the house. I followed, avoiding the gaping
holes in the floor. The inside was in even worse
shape than the outside. Half the ceiling had collapsed, revealing ancient lathing. The horsehair
plaster walls were riddled with cracks, and the
two ancient light fixtures on the chimney walls
dangled from frayed electric wires that Edison
would have rejected as out of date. I stared at
all this desolation as Peggy perched on the arm

of a mouse-chewed Victorian sofa surrounded by litter.

"What are you going to do with it?" I asked.

"Turn into a do-it-yourself freak. I've got a loan from the bank and I'm going to have an absolute ball. I've always wanted to take a wreck like this and really do a job on it. Jeff's going to help me. That is, when he's not with you." She paused. "You see, I'm filing for a divorce. And it's not just because of Charlotte Dreyfus."

An awkward pause.

"I thought you wanted to try to make it work?"

"I did, at first. But while you were away, I said, 'Peggy, you're a dope. You've had a good eighteen years, but face it—you've never liked politics. You have a successful real estate business. Your husband has gone off after another woman. Why the hell are you trying to hang on to him?' And the answer was simple: I don't know why. So I'm not." She got up from the sofa and looked around the room. "Anyway, I wanted you to see this place. It's a mess now, but it's going to be beautiful."

I started laughing.

"I'm glad you think it's funny."

"It's not funny. It's . . . I don't know. Charlotte doesn't want me, you don't want me . . . God, I feel like a plague victim!"

"You'll survive. You men generally do."

She came over to me and put her hand on my cheek. "It was a good eighteen years, Bill. Let's not spoil them with a bad ending."

I considered trying to change her mind, but decided against it. After all, she was right and I knew it. It was over.

"Shall we go home?" she said. "I'll fix some dinner . . ."

I followed her out of the house, thinking, for the first time in eighteen years, I wasn't sure where "home" was.

Chapter
15

That night we discussed the details of the divorce. It was all very civilized. Peggy had some money of her own, and though she was in a position to put me over a financial barrel, she didn't, for which I was grateful. The house was ours jointly, but I told her she could have my share of it if I could stay until she moved out to the new farm. She agreed. Jeff would divide his time between us pretty much as he wished, and that arrangement went smoothly. In fact everything went too smoothly. I found it hard to accept that after eighteen years of one's life there didn't seem to be anything left to fight over.

That night I slept on a sofabed in the small downstairs room that doubles as a library and my West Schuyler office. As I lay in the dark, staring at the ceiling, I thought of Charlotte. At first my bitterness toward her increased. It was all *her* fault. My political troubles, my divorce. One woman had undone my life. Unfair, but to be expected considering my mood. But as the clock ticked on I began to think of the other Charlotte—not that harridan who'd invaded my hospital room that morning but the Charlotte I had fallen in love with. The more I thought, the more I wanted that Charlotte and the more I realized how much I had been in love with her. I kept repeating to myself I *couldn't* have been that wrong about her. Certainly being the wife of an upstate lawyer probably held little appeal for her, but still . . . there had been so much warmth between us, and this morning it had vanished. It seemed unreal that a brawl with a reporter could have killed it.

I turned on the light, sat up and looked at the clock. Midnight. To hell with it. I had to talk to her. I picked up the phone and dialed her apartment. The phone rang five times. I had about decided she was out, when it was answered.

"Hello?"

It was a male voice. I said nothing.

"Hello?" the voice repeated irritably. "Is anyone there?"

I put the phone down. I turned out the light. Well, that was *that*. A rich, beautiful woman like Charlotte Dreyfus had a whole cityful of available men, and I had been, as usual, incredibly shortsighted to think I was *the* one.

Love? As she'd said, sex in the bathtub. I thought of Nicky's beautifully innocent statement that love was the most important thing in the world.

Not her mother's world.

The next morning I drove to the cabin on the lake and locked myself away from the world for ten days. It was good therapy. I fished a little, swam a lot, caught up on my congressional homework, read *All the President's Men* and a couple of novels, fought mosquitoes and spent a happy half hour watching a frog on a rock. I felt like a kid again, and it made me feel better. I tried to forget Charlotte, and tried not to think of Nicky. I knew her six weeks were almost up. I wanted to see her but there was no way to do it without also encountering Charlotte. That I couldn't take. So I did nothing.

The morning of the tenth day I drove back to West Schuyler to find that Nicky had contacted me. In the mail was a printed invitation that read, "United Charities and Dreyfus House Invite You to a Gala Amateur Hour." The Gala

Amateur Hour was to be held the following Sunday. at Dreyfus House, tickets were ten dollars, the proceeds were to go to United Charities, and the cost was tax deductible. Scrawled across the invitation in blue ink was the message: "You *promised*. Nicky."

I knew what she meant. I had promised to go with her to the hospital at the end. Now the end was near, and she was reminding me. She knew what had happened between her mother and me, knew why I was staying away and must have decided to try and see me at Dreyfus House.

Even if it meant running into Charlotte, I knew I had to keep that promise.

Sunday was a cold, gray early-autumn day. I climbed the steps of the brownstone along with a crowd of ticketholders, most of them in their thirties and early forties. From snatches of their conversation I gathered many of them had kids in the show, and I wondered if Nicky was going to perform. Socially it was a mixed bag —some were Upper-East-Side Young Parents wrapped in trendy furs. Others looked suburban, some as if they hailed from Queens. As I was waiting to squeeze through the door I spotted the maroon Rolls-Royce pulling up to the curb, the Rolls that had been my sparring partner that night two weeks before. I pushed out of the crowd going into Dreyfus House to watch Clyde get out and open the back door of the limousine.

Out stepped Charlotte. She was wearing a black
mink and a smart hat: as always, I was jolted
by her smashing looks. But when I saw her face,
something else jolted me. It looked pale and much
thinner. What she was going through with
Nicky showed.

She wasn't going through it alone. A man
got out of the car behind her. He was wearing a
Chesterfield and a well-cut dark blue suit. He was
powerfully built, tall and good-looking in a rather swarthy way—like a Marlboro Man gone
Wall Street. Feeling urges of latent violence toward my successor, and not wanting Charlotte
to see me, I squeezed into the brownstone,
bought a ticket at the rudimentary box office
that had been set up in one of the side rooms,
then made my way down the hall to the big
room in the back where, it seemed so long ago,
Charlotte had shown me her art students and I
had gawked at Juanito's sister.

Now the room was transformed. A curtain
had been strung across it, cutting off a third of
it for a stage and dressing-room area, leaving
two-thirds of it for folding chairs. The makeshift
auditorium was filling, and I looked around for
Nicky. She wasn't there, and since she hadn't
come with her mother I figured she probably
was going to be part of the show. I gave my
ticket to a young usher who handed me a program. Then I took a seat in one of the rear
corners and looked at the program.

The Gala was a joint effort of several city

and suburban schools—public and private—and
as I ran down the list of acts, there it was: "Pas
de deux from the 'Nutcracker' by Tchaikovsky"
read act number seven. "Danced by Miss Nicole
Dreyfus and Mr. Eugene Miller." I remembered
the night at the ballet in San Francisco when
she had cried at the end of the performance. I
remembered thinking that her tears were
caused by the realization that she would never
dance on a stage. Well, Nicky had fooled me.
She was going to dance. Not much of a stage,
admittedly, and not exactly the Bolshoi or Kirov,
but a stage, nevertheless. Moved as I was by the
thought of her private victory and eager as I
was to see her dance (I had no doubt she was
good), I couldn't help but wonder how she could
manage it physically. Certainly now, in the last
days, she could hardly have the stamina to perform a difficult dance in public. . . .

Charlotte and her escort came into the
room. I watched as they found two empty chairs
on the other side from me. They sat down and
looked at their programs. After a moment Charlotte put the program down and looked around
the room. She saw me. She looked a little surprised, I think. We stared at each other. Then
she turned away and looked at the stage curtain.
That was all. No sign of anything but brief surprise.

Ten minutes later, the room filled to over-
flowing (there were standees), green blinds were
pulled over the windows, two spots hit the

curtain, and a gray-haired lady who taught "Dramatics" at one of the participating schools came out. In high, pear-shaped tones she thanked everyone for their interest and their contributions. Then she introduced the first act. It was Mary Beth Schwartz from a Queens high school. A recording of "The Flight of the Bumblebee" buzzed out of two loudspeakers, the curtains opened, and there on the small stage was Mary Beth, dressed in red spangled tights and a green top hat, twirling a big silver baton. Mary Beth was billed as "Baton-Twirler Extraordinaire." She dropped her baton twice, and her top hat fell off once. Polite applause, then on to the next act.

Which was Arnold Freeman, a junior from White Plains High, who gave impersonations of Judy Garland, Marlene Dietrich and Tallulah Bankhead, including "Falling in Love Again." The audience was kind.

Next came two teenagers from Manhasset, who sang the first act love duet from "Madama Butterfly." They were surprisingly good, the audience responded well and I began to think that Nicky had a chance, after all. I remembered her mirrored practice room, her Pavlova poster, her Tchaikovsky T-shirt, her "Dying Swan" bit. How I wanted the audience to be receptive to her. How I wanted it all to be beautiful for Super-Brat's last bow.

The next act was the P.S. 82 Madrigal Singers, and as they tra-la-la-ed their way through

"My Love Deigneth to Pluck Me a Rose," I saw Juanito pushing his way through the crowd toward Charlotte. Finally reaching her, he whispered something. She in turn whispered to her friend and they both got up to start out of the room. If that hadn't been enough to tell me what had happened, the distant ambulance siren would have. As its mournful wail grew louder, almost drowning out the madrigal singers, I got out of my seat to make my way to the exit. Super-Brat was being robbed of her last bow, and it was time for me to keep my promise.

I had just reached the door when I heard the lady with the pear-shaped tones announcing that Miss Nicole Dreyfus would not be able to dance the pas de deux "because of illness."

Chapter
16

When I reached the front door I saw Charlotte's limousine pulling away. Spotting Juanito, I asked him what had happened.

"Nicky collapsed," he said. "She twisted her ankle two days ago rehearsing for the show. Nobody thought it was serious, but it must have gotten infected or something because about twenty minutes ago she fainted."

"Did they take her to a hospital?"

He nodded and told me which one. I thanked him and went out onto the street to find a cab. It was raining lightly now. There was a sur-

prising amount of traffic for a Sunday afternoon, so it took me almost ten minutes to get a
taxi. As we drove to the hospital I told myself
how wrong it was to take her to one of those
way-stations to the next world. I remembered
how frightened she was of hospitals. Wasn't it
cruel to force her into the cold antiseptic world
she hated so much? Wouldn't it have been better to take her home and let her stay in her
room, that crazy room filled with horror movie
posters and King Kong and Mr. Spock, that room
that somehow was so right for this crazy,
spoiled, over-sophisticated and yet really wonderfully innocent little girl that I adored? And
I did adore her.

It took twenty minutes to get to the hospital.
I was directed to the third floor by the receptionist. When I got off the elevator I saw Charlotte's friend in the small visitors' reception
area. He was talking to a nurse, and when I
heard his voice I thought I recognized it as the
voice that had answered the phone in Charlotte's
apartment the night I called her from West
Schuyler. Then I heard the nurse say, "All right,
doctor," and she clicked down the white corridor.

He noticed me looking at him, so I came
over to introduce myself.

"I'm Bill Dalton."

"Oh yes. Nicky's talked about you a good deal.
My name's Roger Silliphant. I'm Nicky's doctor."

As we shook hands he must have thought
I was a halfwit the way I was staring at him.

It wasn't the time or the place to ask what I then asked, but I couldn't help it. "Doctor . . . were you in Charlotte's apartment one night about two weeks ago?" I said, feeling totally stupid.

He looked justifiably confused. "I might have been. Why?"

"Someone called and you answered the phone?"

"Oh yes, I remember. The person hung up. Was that you?"

"Yes."

"Charlotte had called me because Nicky was running a high fever. She was upset about something that had happened that morning . . ." He paused. "As a matter of fact, she was upset about you. She was angry at her mother because apparently you two had had some sort of argument. I was just leaving the apartment when you called. Why did you hang up?"

"I thought I had the wrong number," I lied. My mind was whirring like a computer gone haywire. He was the doctor, not the lover? The doctor-lover? No, no. The *doctor*. I'd apparently jumped to conclusions all over the place—

"Do you want to see Nicky?" he asked.

"Yes. They said she'd hurt her ankle?"

"Well, actually she did. She insisted on being in the show, and I told Charlotte I didn't see how it could make much difference. One peculiarity of what she has is that the patient *can* function almost to the end. But then, all it takes is a minor injury—a bump, a hurt toe, or in this case a twisted ankle—and then infection sets in and the blood can't fight back. Technically what's going to kill her is pseudomonas septicemia. Actually, of course, it's the cancer."

The word "kill" did it. It was the end, after all.

"How long?" Two words I didn't want answered.

"A few hours. We're pumping antibiotics into her but it's pointless. There's nothing we can do. We haven't been able to do anything for about six weeks."

I looked down the hall. "Which is her room?"

"Four. Her mother's in with her now. Shall I tell her you're here?"

I nodded, and he went down the hall to enter the room. I waited. At risk of sounding cruel, I remember that as I stood in that sterile visitors' "area" with its vinyl chairs and out-of-date issues of *Field and Stream,* I kept thinking that for Nicky's sake I wanted it to be over. For anyone so full of life, every minute in the hospital had to be torture. Yes, life is sacred. But for Nicky, at this point, death might be a relief.

Dr. Silliphant came back into the hall and motioned to me. As I walked to him, Charlotte also came out of the room.

"Nicky wants to see you," she said. "I know what she's going to tell you, but don't believe it."

With that, she went back to the visitors' area, followed by Silliphant. I had no idea what she was talking about.

The door was ajar. I pushed it open and went in. Standard hospital room. A vase of fresh flowers on the bureau. Standard hospital bed. Window blinds pulled down. Nicky in the semi-dark, an inverted bottle on a stand next to the bed pumping fluid through a tube into a vein in her left arm.

What wasn't standard was the TV set on the wall over the bureau. It was on, and a movie was playing, though the sound was so low as to be almost inaudible.

"It's 'The Mummy's Hand,'" I heard her say. "They're just boiling the tana leaves to bring him to life. Got any tana leaves for me?"

I didn't want to cry.

"Afraid not, Super-Brat."

I came to the bed and looked at her. She was half propped up. She looked extremely pale and even thinner, but still she looked beautiful. She reached her free hand out and took mine.

"You know," she said, "you're a real jerk."

Her voice was weak, but still full of life.

"Probably. What did I do now?"

"You believed that junk Mother told you. About not wanting to marry you because you'd blown the Senate."

"She told you?"

"I got it out of her—finally. She got the idea out of some old Joan Crawford movie—I would have spotted it in ten seconds."

"What idea?"

She sighed.

"You're so *dumb*, but I guess people in love don't act smart. That morning, after you got in the fight with the reporters, your campaign manager—what's his name?"

"Tony."

"That's him. He called Mother and told her if she married you, your career would be over. So she decides to be noble, like Joan Crawford or something. And she goes to see you and acts tough so you'll stop loving her and then you'll go back to your wife and be a senator and all that gunk. It was really a dumb idea. But the dumbest thing is that it worked. You *believed* her. How could you have done that? I told you she was super-fantastic. I may have a lot of faults but I never lie."

I didn't answer, I didn't know what to say.

"Well, it's *true*," she insisted. "She really *does* love you. And now she's back on Valium and she's going to go bananas. You've *got* to take care of her. You don't have to marry her if you don't want to, but you've got to take care of her. Will you?"

I nodded.

"You promise?"

"I promise. I promised I'd be here, didn't I?"

She seemed to relax.

"Yes." She looked at me a moment, then said, "Did you really think *I'd* have a creep for a mother?"

I smiled.

"I guess I didn't *really* believe it."

She shook her head.

"Joan Crawford. Too much."

She looked back at the TV set.

"Look," she said. "Kharis is coming to life!"

"Who's Kharis?"

"The mummy. He drank the tana leaves and now he goes out to get the archeologist who broke the sacred seals of his tomb. I know *all* the plots. 'Nicky Dreyfus, who knew all the plots to all the old movies.' What a great way to spend your life."

I squeezed her hand.

"I can think of worse ways."

"I guess I can too." She thought a moment. "I wish I could change the ending to *this* plot. I wish the doctor would come in and say, 'Guess what, Nicky? We made a boo-boo. All you have is a cold.'"

A nurse came in the room.

"How's Nicky?" she asked.

"Oh, super."

The nurse signaled to me. I let go Nicky's hand and went over to her. She whispered something about "... the doctor says ..."

"I know."

She left the room, and I went back to Nicky. She was watching me.

Then she extended her free arm, and I leaned down and hugged her. She hugged me back.

"I wish you'd been my real father," she whispered.

"I do too."

"Will you remember me?"

"Always."

We held on to each other a moment more. Then she let go and I straightened up. We looked at each other.

"Goodbye, Super-Brat. I love you."

She nodded slightly. I went to the door, looked back and blew her a kiss. But she didn't see it. She had turned back to watch the TV set.

In the ghostly blue-white light from the screen I could see tears running down her face.

I left the room and closed the door softly. Tears were running down my face too.

The funeral was held two days later in a cemetery on Long Island. I had said little to Charlotte when I came out of Nicky's room, not only because it wasn't the time or the place, but also because I wanted time to think. I believed what Nicky had told me. She was right when she said she never lied—particularly about something as important to her as her mother—and the more I thought about it, the angrier I got at Tony. I called him. After I'd badgered him, he finally admitted he had called Charlotte the morning after the fight.

"And just what the hell did you say to her?"

"That if she married you, it would be the kiss of death. It still is, if you're thinking of changing your mind."

"I am. And I'm not so sure you're right.

But if you are—if the voters don't like me because of Charlotte—then the voters are going to lose one damned good senator."

He thought about this a moment.

"Well, maybe we can arrange a tie-in. If the candidate's wife gave out free samples of her face cream at the polls . . ."

I didn't laugh.

At the funeral, I kept my distance during the brief service. I'm not sure why. Maybe it was because I didn't want to see the box go into the ground, or maybe it was because I wanted to leave Charlotte alone with her grief. Only when she walked away from the gravesite did I go over to her. She stopped when she saw me.

I waited a moment, then said, "She was something special."

She nodded slowly.

"I believed her, you know."

"You shouldn't have," she replied. "My way's a lot smarter."

"No one ever said people in love act smart."

Her face, which had been so tense, almost relaxed into a smile.

"That sounds like something Nicky would say."

"She did."

I took her hand then, and we walked from the gravesite together.

ABOUT THE AUTHOR

FRED MUSTARD STEWART'S previous novels include *The Mephisto Waltz, The Methuselah Enzyme, Lady Darlington* and *The Mannings.* A graduate of Princeton, he is a native of Anderson, Indiana, and presently makes his home in Connecticut.

"I fell in love with these women's story . . . if you like family sagas, do yourself a favor and read *Traditions*."

—Cynthia Freeman, author of *No Time for Tears*

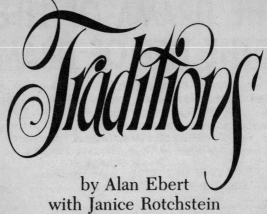

Traditions

by Alan Ebert
with Janice Rotchstein

Through love and loss . . . through tragedy and triumph . . . through three remarkable generations . . . they were a proud family bound by *TRADITIONS*.

Read *TRADITIONS*, on sale December 15, 1982, wherever Bantam paperbacks are sold or use this handy coupon for ordering:

Bantam Books, Inc., Dept. TR, 414 East Golf Road, Des Plaines, Ill. 60016

Please send me _____ copies of TRADITIONS (22838-2 * $3.75). I am enclosing $_____ (please add $1.25 to cover postage and handling, send check or money order—no cash or C.O.D.'s please).

Mr/Ms_____

Address_____

City/State_____ Zip _____

TR—11/82

Please allow four to six weeks for delivery. This offer expires 5/83.

DISCOVER
THE DRAMA OF LIFE
IN THE LIFE OF DRAMA

☐	21030	**CYRANO DE BERGERAC** Edmond Rostand	$1.50
☐	21040	**FOUR GREAT PLAYS** Henrik Ibsen	$2.25
☐	13615	**COMP. PLAYS SOPHOCLES**	$2.95
☐	22955	**FOR COLORED GIRLS WHO HAVE CONSIDERED SUICIDE WHEN THE RAINBOW IS ENUF** Ntozake Shange	$2.95
☐	22640	**MODERN AMERICAN SCENES FOR STUDENT ACTORS** Wynn Handman	$3.95
☐	14257	**SAM SHEPARD: SEVEN PLAYS** Sam Shepard	$3.95
☐	20963	**THE NIGHT THOREAU SPENT IN JAIL** Jerome Lawrence and Robert E. Lee	$2.50
☐	14964	**BRIAN'S SONG** William Blinn	$2.25
☐	20971	**THE EFFECTS OF GAMMA RAYS ON MAN-IN-THE-MOON MARIGOLDS** Paul Zindel	$2.50
☐	20777	**50 GREAT SCENES FOR STUDENT ACTORS** Lewy Olfson, ed.	$2.95
☐	22893	**INHERIT THE WIND** Lawrence & Lee	$2.50
☐	21060	**EURIPIDES Ten Plays** Moses Hadas, ed.	$2.50
☐	20657	**THE CRUCIBLE** Arthur Miller	$2.50
☐	14043	**THE MIRACLE WORKER** William Gibson	$2.50
☐	14101	**AFTER THE FALL** Arthur Miller	$2.50

Buy them at your local bookstore or use this handy coupon for ordering:

Bantam Books, Inc., Dept. EDH, 414 East Golf Road, Des Plaines, Ill. 60016

Please send me the books I have checked above. I am enclosing $_____
(please add $1.25 to cover postage and handling). Send check or money order
—no cash or C.O.D.'s please.

Mr/Mrs/Miss_____

Address_____

City_____State/Zip_____

EDH—12/82

Please allow four to six weeks for delivery. This offer expires 6/83.